The UNKINDNESS Of RAVENS

JOHN RYLAND

This is a work of fiction. Names, characters, places, and incidents are products of the author's imagination or are used fictitiously and are not to be construed as real. Any resemblance to actual events, locations, organizations, or persons, living or dead, is entirely coincidental.

World Castle Publishing, LLC
Pensacola, Florida
Copyright © John Ryland 2022
Paperback ISBN: 9781960076007
eBook ISBN: 9781960076014
First Edition World Castle Publishing, LLC, December 20, 2022
http://www.worldcastlepublishing.com
Licensing Notes
All rights reserved. No part of this book may be used or reproduced in any manner whatsoever without written permission, except in the case of brief quotations embodied in articles and reviews.
Cover: Karen Fuller
Editor: Karen Fuller

Chapter One

Miranda picked her way through the woods, following the sound of beating wings. Her eyes washed across the canopy that towered above her. Patches of hazy gray sky peeked through, reminding her of the overcast day. She didn't like cloudy days, they always left her feeling sad and lonely.

On days when the sun hid from her and her parents were away at work and she was alone, the hours crept by with a maddening slowness. The house was still and silent, and she could barely breathe. Her mind liked playing tricks on her, confusing her. Those days were torturous, like today.

It wasn't much better when her parents were home, but at least the house wasn't so quiet, and she wasn't alone with her thoughts.

The woods around her were a calm quiet, but not silent. Beyond the sound of dried leaves crunching under the soles of her sneakers, there was evidence that she was not alone. Birds sang sporadically. Squirrels raced up and down tree trunks, stopping occasionally to bark at her with their high pitched squeaks. Things moved. Leaves rustled in the breeze. The forest was alive, unlike her house.

As she breasted the ridge, she leaned against the rough bark of a pine tree to catch her breath. She'd seen the bird land in this very tree, but looking up, she discovered it gone again.

To her right, the hillside fell away steeply, a carpet of leaves descending a hundred feet or more through the trees. What might have been a creek wove its way along the valley floor. She could almost hear the sound of running water. In the heat of summer, the creek was little more than a trickle.

As she turned to her left, the sun broke through the haze, stripping the veil from the forest. As the brighter light filtered through the trees, she glimpsed a color that didn't belong. In the distance, a small spot of light blue stood out amongst the dried leaves. Her head fell to the side, her brow furrowing curiously.

Miranda lifted her eyes slowly, searching the treetops above her for any sign of the bird. She'd followed it from her own back yard to this tree in hopes of escaping the doldrums of her house but now wondered if it had led her here.

Black birds were often seen as an omen or a charmer in some cultures. Was this one either of those? Or just a stupid crow?

She sighed, returning her attention to the splash of color as she started down the gentle rise. Ahead of her, the hill leveled off for about fifty feet, creating a shelf before dropping off sharply like the opposite side of the ridge. On this shelf, the trees thinned considerably, allowing the sun access to the leaf litter on the ground.

She walked slowly, keeping her eyes on the color, watching it weave in and out of her view as she moved from tree to tree. Her pulse quickened with each step. It might not be anything, but then again, it might be something interesting.

Her eyes went to the canopy again, searching for the bird. Surely it had led her here for a reason. It had stood squawking on their back fence until she'd come outside. When it saw her, it flew to a nearby tree. When she followed, it flew into the forest.

Half-way down the incline, Miranda stopped suddenly. He was thirty feet away, laying on his back with his arms folded across his lap the way people did at a funeral. But there was no casket, and he was deep in the woods. He was alone.

Miranda looked around, suspecting a prank or something. Her eyes narrowed as she searched the trees. The forest was silent. The air still. There was no one else around. Her eyes scanned the treetops again, finding no sign of the bird.

Looking back at the boy, she considered the notion that he might simply be sleeping. Perhaps he'd also been led here by the same bird or another. Maybe he'd gotten tired and laid down for a nap.

She sat on the ground, pulling her knees to her chest, and watched from a distance. If he awoke, she'd have enough of a head start to escape easily. She had all day. She could wait him out.

It's a peculiar thing to do, she thought. To sleep in the woods like this. Just laid out on the ground without a care in the world. Miranda's brow creased as she studied him. Her eyes straining to see if his chest was moving, if he were breathing. From this distance, she couldn't tell.

She sat and watched him until her butt ached. By then, she'd collected three mosquito bites, and the seat of her shorts were damp from the ground.

Deciding that it was time to put up or shut

up, she stood slowly and let out a loud sigh. She hoped he'd hear her and wake up. When that didn't work, she cleared her throat.

When her efforts drew no response, she moved a little closer, getting a better view of him. His eyes were closed beneath a tangle of sandy brown hair. A smattering of freckles danced across the bridge of his nose and onto his cheeks. A half dozen stray leaves lay on his chest like he'd been here for a while. His jeans were dirty and well-worn. A dirty knee peeked from a hole in the left pant leg. On his feet were a pair of battered, off brand sneakers, with no socks.

His cheeks were sunken slightly, pale, and colorless. Thin lips held only the whisper of pink. He looked peaceful, though, like he was enjoying a good dream. There were no signs of an injury, no scrapes, or bruises. There was no blood.

A hand went to her forehead as her vision blurred. Miranda felt herself moving toward the boy but couldn't hear the leaves crunching beneath her feet. In her mind, she was no longer in the woods. She was walking through a child's nursery.

There were shadows. All was still and quiet. In the early morning gloom, she could just make out the jungle motif. To her left, the painting of a brown and yellow giraffe peeped over a rocking chair. Protrusions stuck out of the top of his head like spaceman antennae. It had a big smile on its face and blue eyes. To her, it didn't look like a very realistic giraffe at all.

To her right, a crib sat bathed in the soft glow of a nightlight. On the wall above the crib, a lion and a zebra looked down into the bed. Mortal enemies, predator and prey, come together to adore the babe. Beside the bed, a hippo splashed in a pool of water. It wasn't looking at the baby at all, but it did look rather happy about something.

Her bare feet moved across the carpet, bringing her to the crib. The baby inside was still, tucked beneath his warm blankets. His face was peaceful, like he was having a good dream. She wondered what babies dreamed about. Did they dream at all? She pushed an arm through the wooden bars on the side of the crib. She just wanted to touch him, to hold his hand. It was so little, like a doll's.

As her fingers touched the baby's hand, Miranda's eyes flew open. She gasped, finding herself back in the woods and standing next to the body. Her brow wrinkled as she spared a glance back up the slope. She didn't remember walking here.

Her eyes darted to the canopy. She did remember following the bird. She remembered seeing the blue color through the trees and standing on the slope. She remembered sitting in the leaves but not walking to the body.

She pursed her lips and sighed through her nose. This wasn't the first time it had happened. She'd see things in her mind, weird things that didn't make sense. Every time she'd end up somewhere other than where she started.

Most of the time, it was minor, lasting only a few seconds. If anyone else were around when it happened, they didn't seem to notice. Her body kept doing what it was supposed to be doing, but her mind would check out. Once, her mother was talking to her when it happened. When Miranda came back, her mother was staring at her, awaiting the answer to an unheard question. She'd gotten mad because Miranda wasn't listening.

Another sweep of the canopy revealed no sign of the bird. Miranda swallowed hard and licked her lips as her eyes came back to the body. "Hey, you." No reply came. She pursed her lips, studying him more. "Hey, kid." She bumped his left foot with the toe of her shoe. A couple of flies rose from him and buzzed noisily past her face. She swatted at them as they went, never taking her eyes off the kid.

Miranda stepped back. Both hands rose to her head as the world began to swim again. She closed her eyes, and a voice leapt forward from the dark recesses of her mind.

Ain't he a dandy?

Miranda bent forward, her palms pressed to the sides of her head. Suddenly flowers were everywhere. The air was perfumed with their scent. A sea of beautiful flowers surrounded a tiny white coffin. There was a bald man in a black suit standing behind the flowers. The man held a book high in the air, shaking it as he spoke, his voice full and resonate. He sounded like he was used to talking to people.

"When life visits such atrocities upon us as this, it is the result of a fallen and broken world. The loss of innocence cannot be recompensed. The indignity of suffering knows no bounds but revels in its own unkindness."

Unkindness. Miranda cringed as the word echoed through her mind, followed by a woman's voice, loud and shrill.

Ain't he a dandy?

Miranda opened her eyes, finding herself in the forest again. The color drained from her face as a realization descended upon her. The kid wasn't sleeping. He was dead.

She stared at him a long time while the depth of the truth settled on her. Her mind screamed for her to run, to hurry home and climb into bed, to pull the covers over her head and pretend she didn't see this dead kid.

Like last time.

Her head jerked around, expecting to find someone behind her. When she saw no one, her brow creased with confusion. The last line had come to her in a whisper, like someone was telling her a secret that everyone else already knew.

She gasped as a large black bird landed gently half-way across the clearing. It looked at her, its dark eye surveying this strange girl. Its dark beak open slightly as if to speak. The sun shimmered off the feathers along its back.

Shaking her head, Miranda turned back to the body. Her mind told her to go, but she stayed. This was a kid. Maybe eight or nine. He was younger than her, and he was dead. The unnaturalness of a dead kid paralyzed her. Kids weren't supposed to die. Old people, yes. Grownups, sometimes. But not kids. Kids weren't supposed to die.

But sometimes they do. Don't they?

The whisper was back, but this time she didn't bother to turn around. She knew the bird would be there, staring at her.

Her head tilted to one side as she stared at the body, wondering if he were a nice kid or not. She wanted him to be a jerk or a bully. The kind of kid who'd sneak up behind you and pull your hair, then run away laughing, especially if he made you cry. The kind of kid who'd take your stuff, break your pencil, or knock your books out of your hand. If he were that kind of kid, maybe it wouldn't be so bad.

But he wasn't that kind of kid.

Her lip began to quiver as she looked at him. He wasn't a jerk or a bully. Not this kid. He looked like a nice boy. Now he was dead and alone in the woods. Kids weren't supposed to die, but sometimes they did.

Sometimes they did.

She sat on the ground and crossed her legs, studying him further. He didn't go to her school, or at least she'd never seen him. But he had to go to school somewhere, didn't he? Yes. He went to school, he did math and took spelling tests. He ate lunch with his friends. He did homework and probably got yelled at by his parents, just like she did sometimes.

He was just a kid like her, but he was dead, and she wasn't.

Ain't he a dandy?

But how did he get here? There'd been no Amber Alerts about a missing kid lately. Actually, there hadn't been one all summer. Those always got big air-time. There would have been volunteers and a search party. She'd have known about it.

If there wasn't a missing kid report, that meant that no one was looking for him. That meant that someone probably knew he was missing and just didn't care. A kid didn't just die without his parents knowing it, did they?

No. They didn't.

That probably meant someone had put him here and didn't want him found. Someone had thrown him away like a broken toy or a sock with a hole in it. He'd been discarded.

Her heart ached at the word.

She sat in silence, considering the unfairness of his situation. The unkindness. She sat and wondered how he died and what his name was as the shadows of dappled sunlight crept across the body.

Ain't he a dandy?

She squeezed her eyes shut against the voice in her head.

In the end, it didn't matter how he'd died. Dead was dead. He was dead. But what was his name? As she stared at the body, a name swam forward in her mind. Andy. Her head fell to the side, aligning her face with his as she surveyed his features. He did sort of look like an Andy. She offered him a smile. "Hello, Andy. I'm Miranda. You don't have to be alone anymore."

Miranda jumped as the forest erupted with a loud, shrill squawk. She looked around, realizing that she'd been staring at Andy for a very long time. Long enough for her legs to become stiff and achy.

    Searching the canopy as she stretched her legs in front of her, she found the bird high in a pine tree. A quick check behind her told her that the bird who'd been there was gone. It was now a hundred yards away, but its size and soot black color stood out against the hazy that had returned to the sky. Her eyes followed it as it took off, gliding effortlessly through the trees toward them. It landed on a limb near Andy, its head pivoting from side to side with quick, jerky movements as it surveyed him with its dark eyes.

    "Aren't you a loud one?" she asked. Her eyes narrowed as she watched the bird. He'd brought her here but was it by plan or accident? Either way, the notion that it couldn't keep a secret began to grow in her mind.

    "You're quite the talker, aren't you?" she asked.

    Her hand rummaged casually beneath the leaves as she spoke, keeping her eyes on the bird. Her fingers found a partially buried rock, and a smile tugged at the corners of her mouth.

Dirt pushed beneath her fingernails as she began digging in the soft, loamy soil. The bird hopped further down the limb toward Andy. "You really mustn't stare. It's quite rude, you know. Didn't your mother teach you any manners?"

The bird stopped, leaning forward as it surveyed Andy, tilting its head to the side. When its head jerked up, looking again at Miranda, it was too late. She'd loosed the rock from the ground and held it in the palm of her hand.

"I don't think so, you nasty bird." She gripped the rock and flung it through the air. The jagged edge hit on the shoulder of its wing, sending it fluttering to the ground. She leapt to her feet and ran to the bird as it flailed in the leaves, squawking incessantly. Before she realized what she was doing, her foot was on its neck. There was a soft crack as bones gave way, and the bird went limp.

"Well then," she said with a sigh as she stared down at it. "That's what you get. You should have kept your mouth shut. Can't have you squawking to everyone in town. Now, can we?" She found a stick and pushed the bird away, tossing it over the edge of the hill and out of sight. She'd never killed anything other than a bug before, but it was unavoidable. The thing was ill-intentioned and had to be stopped.

Going back to her seat, the weight of her situation began to dawn on her. In the back of her mind, she knew the right thing to do would be to tell her parents. But if she did that, they'd call the police. The police would take Andy away. They'd probably bury him in some unmarked grave somewhere, and she'd never even know where it was. He'd be alone, and she'd never see him again.

Her eyes went back to his face, and a thin smile came to her lips. He was a boy that nobody wanted, tossed away. He'd been left alone, but she'd found him. It wasn't the same as finders keepers, but it wasn't completely different either.

Still, she had work to do. There was surely more than one nosey bird in these woods.

Miranda stepped back from Andy's body, surveying the fruit of her labor. He couldn't help it, but the day was warm, and like most other boys she knew, Andy was beginning to stink. The cedar boughs she'd covered him with lent the air a pleasant, piney scent that masked the smell. They would also help protect him from scavengers, like that mean bird. She'd already seen two more of them, but they'd kept their distance.

She armed sweat from her brow with a tired sigh and looked skyward. The sun was getting close to the treetops in the west. The truth that she'd have to leave sent a pang of regret through her heart, but she didn't have a choice. If she weren't home when her parents got back from work, they'd worry. That would complicate things. Plus, she still hadn't tidied the house like she was supposed to.

"I can't stay the night, Andy." She looked at him, nodding sadly. "I know. But it's just for the night. I can come back tomorrow." She turned and started away but stopped. She shook her head without looking back, her face a mask of pain and sadness. "It'll be dark tonight, I'm sorry. I'll bring some candles or something tomorrow. You'll be okay. I promise."

Miranda clenched her eyes, pushing tears from the corners. "I promise."

Miranda found her mother in the living room with a glass of wine in her hand. She was sitting on the sofa with her feet propped on the coffee table. Although she had papers scattered across her lap, her attention was on the shirtless man on the television. As Miranda approached, the shirtless man got down on one knee and took the hand of a young, bikini-clad woman standing next to a pool. It was one of those dating shows that her mother loved, but she wasn't allowed to watch.

"Mom?" she asked timidly.

"Yes, dear." Susan Ploughman found the remote among the clutter and paused the television.

"What's up?"

Miranda shrugged. She'd gone back and forth about telling her parents about Andy. "I don't know." She joined her mother on the sofa, careful not to sit on the papers.

"Something bothering you?"

Miranda shrugged again. "I've got this problem."

"Oh? What kind of problem?"

"Well, it's not really my problem. I've got a friend."

"Oh yeah?" her mother asked, one eyebrow cocked.

"Yeah. They're in a weird spot, and I want to help, but I don't know how."

Susan smiled. "Well, kiddo, I'm gonna need more info than that."

"I'm not sure if I should say just yet." Miranda drew in a deep breath and let it out slowly. "Let's just say they're in a bad spot, and I'm the only one who can help them."

"Well, if they're a friend, you should help. Is

it a close friend?"

"Actually, I just met them."

"That's different, sweetie."

"I know, but I want to do the right thing."

"That's sweet, but if you just met them…." Susan shrugged.

Miranda watched her mother take another sip of wine. "But I'm the only one who can help because I'm the only one who knows this thing about them."

Susan pursed her lips. "Okay, I'll say this. If you feel like you should help, then you should. But you can't allow yourself to get caught up in a situation that will end badly."

Miranda nodded. "I think it's as bad as it will get for this person."

"But not for you?" Susan asked.

Miranda shrugged. "I don't think I'd ever get into any trouble if I helped."

"Okay, then help them out."

"That's just it. I don't know how to help them." She picked at her thumbnail.

"Look, kiddo. You're a good kid. Let your conscience be your guide. Find out what's the best for the both of you and do that."

Miranda nodded, thinking. "Yeah. That's what I'll do."

Susan picked up the remote and unpaused the television. "There you have it, problem solved," she said, her eyes already back on the screen.

Miranda watched the man propose but walked away as the couple kissed. She'd known what she wanted to do about Andy. Her mother had only confirmed it for her. She wouldn't tell anyone about him. Grownups had put him there. Whatever happened to him surely was their fault. If he'd run away or had been kidnapped, there would have been an alert. Adults had failed him, she wouldn't.

Chapter Two

"Good morning, Andy." Miranda shrugged off her backpack, letting it fall to the ground as she scanned the treetops around the clearing. Satisfied that they were alone, she went to the body.

Kneeling, she fanned the flies away as she talked. "I realized last night that I haven't properly introduced myself," she began, rearranging the cedar boughs covering him. "I'm Miranda Ploughman. I go to George Washington Intermediate School. I'm eleven years old. My favorite color is green. Oh, my eyes are green too, but that's not why it's my favorite color."

She went to the backpack and began unloading it onto the ground. "I brought some candles," she produced a clear bag, shaking the small, round candles inside as she held it up for him to see. "There's thirty in here, so if we burn one a night, it'll last a month. That way, it won't be dark, and you won't be so scared."

She reached into the pack again but stopped and looked back at the body. "It's okay. Don't be embarrassed. I'm scared of the dark too. It's nothing to be ashamed of, Andy." She pulled a small stuffed lion from the pack. Its head, surrounded by a bright orange mane, looked too big for the body, giving it a cartoony appearance. The blue eyes and a sappy smile only added to the look.

"I brought you this too. I found it in some old boxes." She crawled to the body and tucked the lion between two branches near Andy's shoulder. "So you don't get lonely. Do you like it?"

She stared at the body for a moment, then smiled. "I thought you might." She turned her attention back to the pack. "Most of the rest is for me," she went on, describing each item as she pulled it from the bag. "A pillow to sit on. A couple bottles of water and some snacks." She pulled a can of Lysol from the bag, sparing a glance at Andy. The cedar boughs helped, but the smell was getting worse.

"I just brought this for the bugs. I know it smells good, but it works for mosquitoes, too," she lied. Holding out her arm, she gave herself a quick spray. She grimaced as the spray coated one of the bug bites she'd been scratching.

"See? Now it's your turn. You know, because of the bugs." She turned the can on the body, saturating the area with the spray. A handful of flies took to the air, buzzing in protest. She tossed the can back into the bag.

"Oh, and I brought this in case any of those nasty birds come too close. I thought they were crows, but I looked then up last night. I think they're ravens. Ravens are bigger and smarter." Her eyes narrowed as she threw a glance toward where the dead bird lay. "And they tend to be more vocal."

Turning back to Andy, she smiled, holding up a slingshot. "I'm actually a pretty good shot with this thing too. My dad taught me." She looked down at the body and shook her head, her smile fading. "I am too. Girls can shoot too, you know."

Miranda crossed her arms over her chest with a "humph," the band of the slingshot dangling over one elbow. "Really?" she asked, one eyebrow arched. "I can't believe you'd say something like that. Would you like to have a little contest to see who's the best shot?" She stared at the body for a moment, then a wry smile slipped across her lips. "I didn't think so."

Turning from him, she placed the pillow at the base of a large oak tree close to Andy. Settling onto it, she leaned against the trunk and stretched her legs out in front of her, crossing them at the ankle. Gripping the sling shot by the handle, she idly flipped the band back and forth while her eyes searched the canopy for birds.

"Oh, just in case you're wondering," she informed Andy, "I'm not going to tell the police about you. They probably wouldn't care anyway." She looked at the body beneath the greenery, wondering if anyone had ever really cared about him at all. "I'm not going to tell anyone about you, I think.

"And before you ask, I'm not some weirdo with no friends. That's not why I'm out here in the woods by myself. I have plenty of friends." She looked at Andy and sighed. "I do," she insisted. "I'm just here because I choose to be here, okay? Now can we change the subject?"

She sat for a moment with her lips pursed and her foot wiggling back and forth rapidly. "Fine," she finally said, shaking her head. "There are a lot of people who call me their friend, but very few that I think of as friends. My parents have friends, and they have kids. They're my friends by default, but I don't like them."

Miranda shook her head. Looking at him, she threw her hands into the air and let them drop to her lap. "Fine. I have no real friends. There, I said it out loud. Are you happy now? I have no friends, and I'm pretty sure my parents hate me."

Her shoulders drooped, and she pulled her knees to her chest. As she stared at the body, her face softened. "Thank you. You're sweet. I think of you as a friend too." She relaxed back against the tree, smiling as she took in the forest around her. "It's really pretty here. It's a nice spot, you know, to be."

She looked at him and sighed, imagining what he was like when he was alive. A smile came to her lips as she thought of him talking to her. In her mind, he had a quiet voice. He'd be the kind of boy who would be caring and attentive. There was a genuineness to him that she liked. He was so unlike anyone else she knew, and she thought that was wonderful.

Relaxing against the tree again, she went back to flipping the sling shot back and forth. The forest was quiet. The day was warm, but the shade was cool. The tension melted from her body, and her eyelids were beginning to feel heavy. When they closed, she didn't fight it. It felt good here. Peaceful. Her mind was quiet.

Finally.

Miranda awoke with a start. She looked around to see what had awakened her and found a raven perched on the toe of Andy's left shoe. She gasped, searching the ground around her for the slingshot. The bird flew onto a low branch, squawking noisily.

"Damn you," she growled, finding the slingshot in the leaves beside her leg. She dug a marble from her pocket and loaded it. Raising the weapon, she aimed and stretched the bands back as far as she could. When she had the bird centered between the uprights, she released the shot. The marble sailed through the air and struck dead center of the bird's chest. It fell from the branch, flapped its wings once, then went still in the dry leaves.

She was smiling when her eyes drifted down to Andy. "See? I told ya," she said, throwing him a wink. She retrieved her kill and carried it to the rise, tossing it next to the one she'd killed yesterday. Dusting her hands, she looked at the two dead birds and shook her head. Her plan would work while she was here, but she couldn't stay all the time. She'd have to make something to keep them away while she was at home.

Going back to Andy, she rearranged the boughs. They were already drying and turning brown. Tomorrow she'd have to get new ones. Their scent had also faded, allowing a pungent aroma to fill the air above him. "Look," she told him, "I'm going to have to leave soon." She paused, then said, "I know, but it can't be helped." She looked around the small clearing. The shadows were getting long. "If I stay too late, my parents might get suspicious. I'm sorry."

Standing, she shouldered the pack. "I'll come back tomorrow. I promise." Her eyes went to the canopy. "We're going to have to figure out something about these stupid birds, though." Looking back at the body, she offered a smile that hid her worry. "Good night, Andy." She started off, making it to the edge of the clearing before stopping suddenly. She dropped the pack and ran back. Tearing open the clear bag, she took out one of the candles. "I almost forgot."

Clearing the leaves next to the body, she sat the candle down and dug a cigarette lighter from her pocket. She lit the candle and stood. "I don't know how long that'll last, but maybe it'll help. Goodnight again." She straightened the stuffed lion, then turned and hurried off, grabbing the pack as she went.

Miranda skidded to a stop as she entered the clearing, gasping in horror. The scene before her was a disaster. She'd heard their squawking and feared the worst but hadn't imagined it would be this bad. More than a dozen ravens were around Andy's body, the cedar boughs pushed aside in their frenzy.

"Get away from him!" she screamed, rushing to the body. The birds protested loudly as they scattered. A wing brushed the side of her face in the confusion. She swatted at the bird, but it was already gone.

One brave raven hopped three feet away from Andy and stopped. Its dark eye darted about, scanning her defiantly. The dark beak opened, and a series of low, guttural croaks came her way.

Miranda stared at it, her body shaking with rage. *How dare you!* her mind screamed. To assault a poor defenseless boy, then not have the decency to flee, to stand shamelessly and squawk at her.

She lunged at it, delivering a kick to its breast as it tried to escape. The blow sent it crashing into a nearby sapling. The bird fell to the ground, one wing hanging askew. It protested with a series of loud grunts and clicks while beating the leaves with its good wing.

Miranda moved toward it, her eyes locked on it. The bravado was gone now as it tried to hop away. She moved quickly, pinning it against the ground. It screeched and tried to bite her when she picked it up, but her free hand shot out and gripped its neck.

"You nasty little bastard," she spat, staring into its dark eye. "What gives you the right?" Gripping the raven's breast in one hand and the neck in the other, she forced it's head around so she could look it in the eye. The bird tried to flail, but she cradled it to her chest, trapping the one working wing.

"You have no right," she said, staring at the dark eye. She twisted the bird's neck until bones crunched beneath her grip. The body went limp.

Turning, she lifted the bird above her head. Her eyes scanned the trees for the rest of its flock. "You see this?" she yelled. "This will be you. This will be all of you!"

She slammed the bird to the ground and went for the sling shot. Lining up a bird, she released the shot. Feathers flew, and the bird dropped from its perch. She worked quickly, getting two more before they finally fled the area.

Grumbling under her breath, she gathered the bodies one by one. Back in the clearing, she considered tossing them over the rise but hesitated.

No, she thought, her chest rising and falling in angry pants. That wasn't enough. She needed to send the rest of them a message. She needed to show them all what would happen if they came back.

Looking around the clearing, her eyes fell on Andy's body, and her anger evaporated. Her shoulders drooped, and the birds dropped from her hands. Her priorities changed with the sight of him. She would teach the birds a lesson, but right now, Andy needed to be looked after.

She dropped to her knees beside the body. In the absence of the cedar boughs, the smell was worse than ever, but she didn't mind. He couldn't help it. It wasn't his fault. If it was anybody's, it was hers for not taking better care of him. She should have done more.

Tears rolled down both cheeks as she looked at Andy. There were bite marks on his face, and holes had been torn in his shirt. Through one of the larger holes, she could see that a patch of gray flesh had been torn away, leaving a gaping, bloodless wound.

"I'm sorry," she whispered as sobs wracked her body. "I'm so sorry."

Miranda stood, stretching her back with a moan. After a cry that lasted longer than she expected, she'd set about securing Andy's body. That meant a trip home and back. She'd doubled the heavy canvass tarp that her father sometimes used for painting and draped his body. Multiple trips to the creek had supplied enough rocks to keep all but the biggest of scavengers from pulling the canvas back. She'd then covered the tarp with leaves, virtually hiding the body from prying eyes.

She looked down at her dirty hands. It was a hard-fought burial but worth every blister and ache. Pride swelled in her chest as she surveyed her work. She couldn't see him anymore, but Andy was safe and secure.

Her eyes lifted to the surrounding trees,

the smile fading from her lips. Anger began to resurface. Now it was time to deal with the scavengers.

They'd been absent during all her work, but she knew they'd come back. When they did, they'd see what happened to dirty birds that messed with her Andy. She'd teach them all a lesson. If that didn't work, she'd kill every last one of them.

Turning from the body, she dug a ball of twine, a hammer, and a handful of loose nails from her pack. She snatched up one of the dead birds and held it before her, shifting it from side to side. Its head flopped listlessly. A thin smile slid across her lips as her eyes narrowed. She'd heard that ravens were smart. If that were true, she'd teach them a lesson they wouldn't soon forget. If they could learn, they'd learn to stay away from her Andy.

Susan Ploughman looked up from her

cooking as Miranda came through the back door. "Hold on a minute, Mama." She lowered the phone from her ear. "Good Lord, sweetie. You're dirty as a stray." She put the wooden spoon down and went to her daughter, brushing a leaf from her hair. "Where have you been?"

Miranda shrugged. "Playing." She looked down, brushing dirt from the front of her shirt.

"Don't do that in the house," Susan sighed, going back to the stove. "Why don't you get a bath before supper. I'll come up in a little bit and brush out your hair." She shook her head, watching her daughter plod out of the kitchen. She raised the phone to her ear again. "Mama, this child has come home looking like a wild animal."

A shrill laugh came through the phone. "You used to do the same thing. You were as bad as your brothers before you got all fancy smancy on us."

"I really doubt that I got as dirty as this one. I should have taken a picture. Lord knows what she's been into."

"You think she's bad? You should have raised boys like I did."

Susan's shoulders fell, struck by the comment. "Really? You just going to say it like that?"

"Oh honey, that's not what I meant. I'm just saying."

"Well, don't, okay?" Susan clenched her eyes, bringing her free hand to her mouth in a fist.

"I'm sorry, sweetie. I didn't mean to upset you."

"It's fine. I mean. No. It's okay, really. Uh, look, I gotta go, okay?"

"I wasn't even thinking."

"Really, it's fine. I gotta finish supper and get Miranda out of the bath. I'll call you tomorrow." Susan lowered the phone, ending the call in the middle of her mother's apology.

Miranda pushed her mother's bedroom door open, finding her sitting on the bed with an open laptop in front of her. "Mom?"

Susan Ploughman slammed the laptop shut, silencing the video, but not before Miranda heard her grandmother's high-pitched voice.

"Hey, sweetie," Susan said, forcing a smile as she hurriedly wiped a tear from her cheek. "I'm sorry. I forgot about your hair."

Miranda froze, taking in the scene. Her mother was upset, but she was trying to hide it. "I, uh…" she tucked the hairbrush behind her back. "It's okay. I was just wondering when supper was."

"I was just going downstairs to finish up, actually." Susan pushed up from the bed and came to the door. "You look much better." She mussed Miranda's wet hair as she squeezed past her. "We eat in ten minutes."

Miranda watched her mother bound down the stairs, then turned back to the laptop on the bed. What was she looking at that upset her so much? She checked the stairs to make sure they were clear, then made her way to the bed. She turned the laptop to her and raised the lid.

"Miranda, sweetie, can you give me a hand setting the table?" her mother called from the bottom of the steps.

Miranda jumped. The lid slipped from her hand and slammed shut. "Coming, mom," she called over her shoulder. She cast another curious look at the computer and sighed. When her mother called her again, Miranda hurried out the door and down the steps.

Chapter Three

Susan Ploughman wolfed down the last of her toast over the sink and washed it down with coffee. She turned, letting out a yelp of surprise when she saw Miranda standing in the doorway in her pajamas, her hair a tangled mess.

"My God, sweetie, you scared me half to death. I thought you were still asleep. Why are you up so early?"

Miranda shrugged as she entered the room. "I set an alarm," she said, opening the refrigerator.

"Why?" Susan asked as she crossed the room to the small mirror hanging next to the mud room door. "You got somewhere to be?" she added with a laugh.

"No," Miranda lied as she poured a glass of orange juice. "I wanted to make sure I got my chores done. Some kids mentioned going to the park later on." She'd been scolded the day before for not straightening the house. She'd slept in and gone straight to see Andy. By the time she got back home, there wasn't enough time to finish.

Susan turned and looked at her daughter, a tube of lipstick sticking out of her raised fingertips. "That's very responsible of you."

Miranda shrugged as she drank.

"I must say that I am very proud of you for taking your chores seriously." Susan turned back to the mirror and applied her lipstick. When she finished, she went to her daughter.

"You're a good kid. How about we do something special this weekend, just us gals?"

"Okay." Miranda forced a smile though she knew they probably wouldn't. Something would "come up." Something always came up.

"Oh crap," Susan exclaimed, glancing at the clock on the microwave. "I gotta go. Traffic is already going to be murder." She mussed Miranda's hair as she passed. "Might wanna run a comb through that before you go anywhere," she called as she hurried toward the back door. "Love you, sweetie."

"Love you—" Miranda's words fell silent as the back door slammed. She sighed and finished her juice alone.

Miranda slid a new roll of toilet paper on the holder and tossed the empty roll into the garbage can next to the toilet. As she stood, she caught her own reflection in the mirror and grimaced.

She picked up her mother's hairbrush and went to work on her hair. When she'd finished, her eyes danced over the army of tubes and bottles of her mother's makeup. She picked a small, round jar and looked at it. Opening it, she sniffed the tan liquid inside. Her nose crinkled, and she closed the lid, setting it aside.

She picked up a tube of her mother's lipstick and opened it. Rolling it out, she puckered her lips and leaned closer to the mirror. Her eyes moved from the reflection of her own lips. She stopped inches from the mirror and stared into her own eyes, searching them.

The eyes in the mirror narrowed. The head tilted to one side. A hand came up, pulling fingertips through her hair. Finally, the eyes closed, and the girl in the mirror was gone.

"Yeah, right," she said, turning from the mirror with a sigh. Shaking her head, she replaced the cap on the lipstick and put it where she'd found it. She walked out of the bathroom without looking back.

Miranda made it halfway across her parent's bedroom before her eyes fell on the picture, stopping her in her tracks.

Her head tilted slightly as she stared at it. The frame was simple but nice. The polished, dark wood had a shiny finish that reflected the light coming through the window behind her. The girl inside the frame held a newborn baby on her lap. The girl was smiling, the baby wasn't.

Miranda moved to the dresser and lifted the picture, looking at her younger self. She didn't remember the day the picture was taken, but it wasn't recent. She was about three years old. Maybe four.

A smile came to her lips as she looked at herself but faded when her eyes drifted to the baby in her arms. He was gone, his short life barely a memory. Her memories of him were like a butterfly. Sometimes they appeared unexpectedly, fluttering around the edges of your mind, only to disappear as quickly as they came.

Everything changed when he came. Everything changed again when he went. Now, her parents were different. Her mother drank a lot of wine. Her dad worked late a lot. Nobody talked about her brother. If they did, they called him "the baby" most of the time.

Miranda shook her head, trying to remember the day the picture had been taken. Shouldn't she remember her baby brother? Shouldn't she be able to remember what happened to him?

"Justin," she whispered, speaking his name for the first time in forever. She drew in a long breath and sighed.

Ain't he a dandy?

Caught off guard by the voice in her head, Miranda winced, dropping the frame. It struck the edge of the dresser and fell to the floor. She gasped, snatching it up quickly. Her fingertips searched the glass for breaks. When she didn't find any, she let out a sigh of relief.

If she'd broken the picture….

Miranda shook her head and placed the frame where it had been. She looked again at the young girl's smile, the vibrance in her eyes, and longed to feel that happy again.

If the baby were only going to stay a short time, why'd he even come in the first place? It would have been better if he'd never come at all.

Stupid baby ruined everything.

Miranda shook her head and left the room, making sure she closed the door behind her. She hadn't thought about the baby in months and wished she hadn't today. She didn't have time for it. She had to finish her chores and see Andy.

"I guess you're right," Miranda agreed. She sat next to Andy with her legs crossed, idly moving leaves around with a stick. "I am melancholy today."

She looked up with a sigh, tossing the stick aside. "I don't know." Turning from Andy, she looked over the clearing. Images of Justin had been popping into her head since she'd seen the picture. She couldn't tell if they were actual memories or if her mind was playing tricks on her again.

It was unusual for her to think of him this often. Usually, it happened every few months. She'd think about him for a few days, then it would stop. She didn't like thinking about him at all.

"I was in my parents' bedroom, and I saw a picture of my baby brother. He died, you know."

Ain't he a dandy?

Miranda grimaced as the voice rocketed through her head. When it was gone, her eyes went to the surrounding trees, finding the ravens that she'd meticulously attached to them. Her feet began to move, bringing her to the closest one.

There were six of them in all, but this was the one who'd led her to Andy. He was also the one who talked too much.

"You're not very talkative today. Are you?" A dry laugh escaped her. "What's the matter? Cat got your tongue?" Hung at eye level with its wings spread, the bird's shriveled eyes stared back at her in silent reproach. "That's probably for the best. I'm in no mood for your bullshit."

Miranda spun and looked back at Andy. "I don't know how he died. Why would you ask something like that?" She moved back to him. "He was a baby. It happens sometimes. I looked it up." She cast her eyes to the canopy, searching for movement. "It's not that uncommon at all, really. I mean, babies die for no reason. There's a name for it, I think."

Her head jerked back around, looking at the raven again. "You!" she growled through clenched teeth. "You just can't keep your trap shut, can you?" She went to the bird again. "Why? Why must you insist on telling lies? Huh?" She stared at it, shaking her head. Her chest rose and fell in angry pants. "I'll show you." She hurried to her pack and retrieved the ball of twine.

Stomping back to the bird, she reached into its mouth and yanked the stick free that had held it open. "You'll never learn," she began as she unfurled a length of twine, snapping it from the spool with her hands. "I've tried to be nice to you," she continued, wrapping the twine around the dark beak. "But did you listen? No. No, you didn't." After she'd made several passes around the beak, she tied it in a double knot beneath it.

Stepping back, she admired her work with

a thin smile. "Now let's see you tell your tales." Her eyes swept over the other birds. Hanging on other trees with their mouths propped open, they looked shocked.

"You all saw it. Don't blame me for this." She stabbed an accusing finger at the raven. "He wouldn't shut up. Blame him, not me."

Turning her back on the birds, she crossed her arms on her chest and scanned the canopy again. "But let this be a lesson to all of y'all. Disobedience will not be tolerated. You are here to warn the others to stay away, not to offer your stupid opinions."

Turning back to them suddenly, she held up the ball of twine, sweeping it back and forth in front of the birds. "Remember, there's plenty of string for all of you."

Miranda walked back to the mound of leaves and collapsed onto her knees. "Don't listen to them, Andy. They're just dumb crows." She looked around slowly with a grin on her face as she studied the birds. She knew they were ravens and that they hated being called crows.

"Anyway," she said, turning back to Andy. "You don't have to worry. I didn't do anything to my little brother." She stared at the leaves, wishing she could see the expression on his face. Not being able to see him made it impossible to know what he was thinking.

"Do you think I did?" she finally asked. One eyebrow began to slide upwards while she awaited a response. Finally, it stopped and returned to normal.

"It's good to know you don't think I'm a killer." A humorless chuckle escaped her. "That would be awkward."

Miranda stirred more leaves with a stick as an awkward silence overcame her. Suddenly she didn't know what to say to Andy. The topic of her brother's death had spoiled the whole day and made her feel worse than ever. Finally, she sighed and tossed the stick aside.

"Look, it's hot, and if you're not going to talk to me, I'm going to go down to the creek and splash around a bit to cool off." She stood, dusting herself off. A sad smile crept across her face. "Don't worry. I'm not going home, and no, I'm not mad at you."

Miranda knelt on a rock and reached her hands into the creek, catching water in them as it spilled over a narrow rock face. The water was cool and refreshing as she splashed it on her face. She collected another double handful and considered having a drink. It was clear and cool.

Deciding against it, she splashed it on her face and pushed her wet hands through her hair. Squatted on the bank, she let her hands hang between her knees as she surveyed the bottom of the hollow. The canopy was thicker down here, lending the air a damp coolness.

Her eyes dropped to the creek before her. No more than a few feet wide, it flowed through the forest unhurried. The bottom was sandy, with a mixture of rocks of all shapes and sizes. She'd seen small minnows a few times, but there were absent today. Wiping water from her forehead with the back of her hand, her eyes followed the trail of the creek.

Movement caught her eye, and she followed a brown leaf as it fell from a nearby tree, drifting gently through the air until it landed in the creek. It barely made a ripple, then, caught by the current, started toward her. With three edges curled upward, it resembled a tiny brown boat. Caught by the water, it moved toward her, a slave to the current. It washed over the ledge next to her and sank in the roiling water. When it finally resurfaced and continued its journey, a smile slipped across her face.

The leaf turned on the twisted and turned atop the water for a few yards, then washed ashore in the eddy behind a big gray rock covered with moss. When the leaf finally sank, her eyes drifted to the dirt alongside the rock. The patch of bare earth was dark and wet. It was the same mud she'd gotten on her hands while retrieving rocks to hold down the tarp covering Andy, but this was darker. Almost black.

Pushing herself up, she went to the rock and dropped to her knees. Leaning over the creek, she found her own reflection in the still water of the eddy. She watched herself drag hair back from her forehead. Staring at the girl in the water, she shook her head, wondering how her life had turned into the mess it had.

Turning from the creek, she found a small pebble. "What are you looking at?" she asked the reflection. When it didn't respond, she tossed the pebble into the water. Her reflection exploded into ripples. She stared at it until the water settled, and her reflection was back.

"I said what are you looking at?" she repeated through clenched teeth. Shaking her head, she balled her hand into a fist. "Shut up," she growled, and slammed her fist into the reflection. It sank into the shallow water, striking a soft patch of black mud.

When she pulled her hand back, her fist

was full of mud. It was cool and sticky, slippery. Raising it to her face, she squeezed her hand into a fist, watching the mud slip between her fingers with a wet squelch.

Smiling, she dropped it and grabbed another handful. Closer to the bank, this batch was firmer but still wet and squishy. Her head fell to one side as she began smearing the mud over her hands, watching the darkness of it cover her skin. When the mud was spent, she gathered more and slowly began working her way over each wrist and forearm.

Holding her hands before her, palms up, she stared at them. The dark mud clung to her skin, covering it in a black, shiny film. Slowly, she raised two fingers to her face. Dragging them across her skin, she left two dark lines across each cheek.

Tilting her head back, her eyes searched the canopy for the birds she was at war with. Finding none, she closed her eyes and smiled.

Chapter Four

Dressed in a pair of black leggings and a matching tee shirt, Miranda moved through the forest with casual ease. Although she was careful not to take the same route to Andy, she'd made enough trips to become familiar with the entire scope of woods that surrounded him. She'd settled into a routine, watching the leaves make their yearly change as the weeks passed. Now, Fall had come, and the trees were dressed in a full array of colors.

The return of school kept her away more

than she would have liked. That made the time she was able to sneak away that much more precious. Luckily, she'd gotten things the way they needed to be to protect Andy. She'd built a small lean-to out of saplings to keep most of the rain out of his face. This wasn't necessary since the old canvas tarp had been replaced with a polyethylene one that wouldn't rot, but every storm had brought the haunting image of rain falling in his face.

Lately, even the birds had become nothing more than an occasional bother. She wasn't sure if it was her message to them that kept them away or if she'd simply killed enough of them to make them wary. Either way, she counted it as a win. When one did show up, she'd kill it and add it to the collection.

Stopping to tie her shoe, she sat and listened to the sounds of the woods. A black and white bird chirped as it flitted about in a tree just ahead of her. She'd looked it up and found it to be an Eastern Chickadee. Somewhere in the distance, a woodpecker was searching for food. Its hammering danced through the forest almost in a whisper.

Smiling, she started to get up but stopped suddenly. A strange noise filtered through the trees. She squatted in the dry leaves, straining her ears. Was it a voice? Surely not. In all the time she'd been coming she hadn't seen so much as a sign of another person.

She gasped, her eyes bulging as the sound came again. Her heart leapt into her throat. It was a voice. Her eyes searched the forest, looking for a color that didn't belong. The voice came again, and she shrank closer to the ground. She wasn't afraid of them seeing her. She could run away, but if they found Andy, they would ruin everything.

Staying low, she crept up a small hill. The voices were moving away from her, but not very quickly. As she crept closer, she could make out two distinct voices. One man, one woman.

She closed her eyes, hoping them a young couple on a romantic stroll. An angry retort from the man vanquished that hope almost as quickly as she had it. She sighed, creeping closer. Now she could clearly make out what they were saying.

"You said you marked it, damn you," the woman snapped.

"Shut the hell up, Brandy. I marked it. I just can't find the mark. It's been a long time."

Miranda's eyes narrowed. They were looking for something, and their general direction was leading them toward Andy. She swallowed hard, a mixture of fear and anger rising in her chest. Were these Andy's parents? Had they left him here alone? Were they the ones that had abandoned him to the elements?

Were they the ones who killed him?

Miranda took in a deep breath, trying to calm herself. The urge to rush out and attack them was strong, but she suppressed it. She wasn't sure who they were or what had happened, but her gut told her they were bad people. She couldn't let them find Andy. She couldn't.

Miranda crawled to the top of the hill. She scurried to cover behind a patch of undergrowth, narrowly avoiding being seen as the woman spun around.

"What was that?" she asked, her wide eyes scanning the woods.

"Shut up. Damn. It's a squirrel, or a deer or some other damned animal that lives out here. Shit, Brandy, you're jumpy as a cat."

"I heard something running through the woods."

"What the hell ever." The man started off again. "You coming or not?"

"I'm coming," she replied, sparing a look over her shoulder at the bush that hid Miranda.

"I don't even understand this whole damned thing anyway. I told you I buried him all proper and everything. Why do you want to see it now? After all this time."

"Just shut up," she growled, rejoining him. "As damned high as you was, I don't trust you."

"Shit, here we go again."

Miranda peeked from behind the bush, watching them argue as they picked their way through the woods. So it was them. The man wasn't just a killer. He was also a liar and a druggie. The fear in her chest subsided, and anger filled the void. As she watched them go, the idea of killing them both began to form in the back of her mind. If she had to, to protect Andy, she would.

When the couple had moved away enough that their voices were faint, she left her hiding spot and followed, moving from tree to tree. The woman stopped and looked back twice but caught up when the man cursed at her for being slow.

With each step they took, they moved closer to Andy, and her pulse quickened. By the time the man stopped, pointing out a skinned mark on a young pine tree, her heartbeat was thundering in her ears. Miranda watched them from behind a tree, struggling to stay calm. Her breaths came in rapid pants, and her palms were sweating.

"It's close by," the man said as he surveyed the area. Miranda let out a sigh of relief when he headed off in the opposite direction of Andy, but it was short lived.

"Hey, dumbass," the woman called in a snarl. "What's that?"

Miranda gasped when the woman pointed directly at Andy. *No!* her mind screamed. She had to distract them, to scare them away. She was wracking her brain when a raven landed in a tree directly above them. It looked down and squawked. The woman jumped, letting out a yelp. Miranda's eyes shot skyward, watching the bird take off from the limb. It was just passing through, but it gave her an idea.

"What the hell was that?" the woman asked, searching the canopy.

"It's just a damned crow," the man complained as he trudged back to her.

Miranda shook her head. He was stupid too. That was good. It would help her plan work.

She worked up some spit in her mouth, then swallowed it to wet her throat. Cupping her hands around her mouth, she did her best impersonation of a crow. It wasn't perfect, but close enough to spook the woman.

"There it is again," she said, spinning to face the sound. "That time, it was over there."

The man threw his arms into the air. "It's a fucking crow. Crows have wings. They move the hell around, you dumbass."

"Don't you cuss me, you asshole."

Miranda smiled, using the noise of the ensuing argument to move to a different tree. As she ducked behind a towering oak, her foot skidded on something, sending her tumbling to the ground. Leaves crunched noisily beneath her as she fell. She recovered quickly and scurried back to the tree.

The woman stopped in mid-sentence, looking in Miranda's direction. "That weren't no damned crow."

The man joined her, and they both scanned the forest.

"I think it was something besides—," she whispered.

He silenced her with a wave of his hand. "Shut up," he whispered. "Let me listen."

Miranda clung to the base of the tree, not daring to look. If they came toward her, she'd hear them long before they got close enough to catch her.

"Well," the man said with a shrug. "Whatever the hell it was, it's gone now."

"Or it wants us to think it's gone," the woman mumbled.

"Look. Do you want to keep looking or what? What was you pointing at?"

Miranda put her hands on the ground to push herself up and found several large acorns. Scooping them up, she stood slowly. The people were talking, so she dared a peek. Their backs were to her, looking toward Andy.

She put one hand alongside her mouth and reproduced the loud call, throwing the acorns at them at the same time. She ducked back behind the tree as the forest erupted with the sound of falling acorns.

"What the shit?" the woman cried, clutching the man's arm.

"That weren't no crow," he said.

"They's somebody out there." she wined. "I know there is."

He spat on the ground and wiped his mouth with the back of his hand. "If they is, they going to regret messing with me. I'll tell you that much." He shrugged the woman from his arm and stepped forward. "Whoever you are, you better get your ass on. I ain't in the mood for playing games."

Miranda smiled from her perch behind the tree. The man was trying to sound tough, but there was an undercurrent of fear in his voice.

"Let's just go," the woman pleaded, tugging on the man's arm.

"Uh uh," he answered. "I ain't gonna listen to your shit another day. We come this far. We seeing it through. Now shut the hell up, and come on."

Miranda listened as they stomped through the leaves. They were moving away from her but toward Andy. She'd only succeeded in delaying them a few minutes. Peeking around the tree, she watched them start down the small rise toward the clearing.

Abandoning stealth, she jumped from behind the tree and raced forward. When she got to the top of the rise above Andy, she stopped.

"What in the holy hell?"

Miranda gasped. They'd found him. Without thinking, she cupped her hands around her mouth and released the loudest caw she could muster. Before the strangers could turn and see her, she ducked and scrambled along the ridge just beyond their view. Twenty feet away, she stopped and let out another screech.

In the clearing, the couple were beginning to panic. The woman, now gripping the man's arm so tightly that her fingertips were white, followed Miranda's path through the forest with her eyes. Every time Miranda let out a screech, she screamed and tightened her grip.

The man was standing in the center of the clearing, looking around, dumbfounded. His eyes bulged when he found the first dead raven. It was nailed to a tree with its wings spread fully. Miranda had shoved a stick into its throat to hold its head up and its mouth open.

"What the hell is going on?" the woman cried, releasing one hand to cover her ear as Miranda let out another screech.

The man's eyes moved to the bird on the next tree, arranged just like the first. Its black feathers had faded slightly, and its eyes were gone from its head. Empty sockets stared back at him. In the woods, Miranda moved again, letting out another screech. His eyes darted around the clearing, finding bird after bird, all nailed to trees and arranged just like the first.

"This is some witchcraft shit," the man said, shaking his head. He found another raven, this one little more than a skeleton and feathers. Miranda screeched again, closer this time, and they both jumped.

"Let's get out of here," the woman pleaded, pulling the man's arm. When Miranda screeched again, tossing more acorns at them, he relented.

They both hurried back up the rise. Miranda moved to the edge of the clearing and began screeching nonstop, and they hurried their pace. She continued until she could no longer hear their clumsy footsteps in the leaves.

Miranda stepped into the clearing with a smile. "Well, now," she said, approaching one of the ravens. She extended a finger, scratching the feathers beneath its beak. "I don't think they'll be bothering us anymore."

Her eyes washed over the birds, each one collected on this very hill when they came to see Andy. They came with bad intentions, but she'd changed their minds and appointed them sentry. They stood guard over Andy, warning the others to stay away. All outsiders, not just ravens.

"Great job, folks. Excellent work." Her head jerked around, looking at the bird next to her. Bands of twine covered his beak almost entirely. They were tied in a bow beneath his chin.

"And what are you mumbling about?" Miranda asked, turning to face the bird. "Why don't you ever shut up? If you hadn't told everyone else about Andy, these guys wouldn't even be here. You should have known better." Her lips pursed tightly as she looked at the bird. "Oh, stop. Those fools aren't going to tell the cops. Geesh, you worry too much. They're drug addicts. The last people they'll go to is the cops." She looked at the bird on the next tree, shaking her head as she jerked a thumb at the bird with the twine on its beak.

Her attention drifted in the direction the people had gone, and she smiled, but it was short lived. The smile faded as her eyes fell on Andy. He was upset.

She rushed to his side and dropped to her knees. "I'm sorry. I know you're sad. It must have been sad seeing them again." She clasped her hands in her lap, nodding.

"I know they were looking for you but not to take you home. They just wanted to make sure no one else could find you and get them in trouble with the cops." Miranda sat in silence for a moment, then shook her head.

"I know what it looked like, but you gotta believe me. I heard them before they got here. He told her that he gave you a proper burial. He lied. He's a stinking liar. He dumped you here. I am the one who buried you."

She wiped a tear from her cheek. "No." After a moment of silence, she said it again. "They're bad people, even if they are your parents. They don't care about you, Andy."

Miranda pushed her hands through her hair as she stood. "I can't believe you'd say that. Look what I've done for you." She threw her hands, spinning slowly as she looked at the circle of birds, at her flock.

"I did all of this to protect you. If it were up to that man, they'd have pecked your eyes out and eaten your guts. I built this for you. You, Andy. Don't you see? Doesn't it even matter?"

Miranda looked at the mound of leaves beneath the shelter and shook her head. "I know you're upset, so I'm going to overlook this. I'm not mad at you." Going to the mound, she fell to her knees. "I protected you." She used the heel of her hand to wipe a tear from her cheek. "I didn't do anything wrong. I didn't."

Miranda looked up at the sky. The shadows would soon be growing, but she couldn't leave right now. Andy was still upset. "It's okay, I'll stay with you. You like the candles, don't you? I'll light one and stay with you." She brushed the spent candle aside and put a new one on the flat rock she'd hauled up from the creek. "See," she said, wiping a tear from her cheek as she lay beside him. "I'll stay as late as I can. It'll be okay. I promise. I won't leave you. I'm here." She patted the stuffed lion half buried in the leaves, shushing him gently. "Everything's going to be okay."

Susan Ploughman threw her arms around her daughter before she could get through the door. "Oh, thank God you're safe." She squeezed Miranda tightly, her arms trembling with relief. "Where in the hell were you?" She added, pushing her daughter to an arm's length. "We were worried sick. It's almost nine o'clock."

"I'm sorry, Mama." Miranda began to cry. "I fell asleep in the park. I'm so sorry." She threw her arms around her mother's waist and hugged her, sobbing.

"Fell asleep?" Susan asked. Looking down at her daughter, she fished a dried leaf from her hair. "There's stuff in your hair. What happened?"

"I'm sorry, Mama."

"Your father is out driving all over the neighborhood. We called all your friends. We were so scared."

"I know. I didn't mean to. I was sitting by a tree and the next thing I knew…." Miranda broke into sobs again. "I'm sorry."

"It's okay, sweetheart. I'm just glad you're okay." Susan hugged her daughter with one hand and dialed her husband's number with the other. "We were so scared."

Chapter Five

Susan hesitated as she pulled her daughter's bedroom door closed, staring at Miranda through the crack. After a hot bath, she had fallen asleep almost at once when she'd laid down. Susan shook her head, her brow creased deeply. She closed her eyes and said a prayer for her daughter, then closed the door.

A pang of regret struck her. She'd been robbed of time that could have been spent with her daughter during her formative years. She tried. It was just so hard to let go of the pain of losing Justin, especially the way they'd lost him.

But hadn't you almost lost Miranda today?

The thought stung, but there was no denying it. They might be here now with no children, having lost them both suddenly. She sighed and rubbed her eyes with her fingertips.

"I don't know," Susan answered, climbing into bed next to her husband. "She's sticking to the story about falling asleep in the park."

"Do you believe her?" Jason asked, his eyebrows raised.

Susan shrugged. "I don't know what to think." She sighed, tossing her hands into the air. "I mean, she's been different lately, withdrawn. I don't know. Something's just not right."

"Do you think she could have been with a boy? She's mentioned this Andy kid a few times." He shrugged. "Do you think they were fooling around?"

Susan gasped. "My God, Jason. She's eleven."

"I know, I know," he said, defensively patting the air with his hands. "I'm just saying."

"No. That's not it," Susan replied sharply, putting the idea to rest.

"Then what is it? You said yourself that she's been acting different lately."

"I don't know what it is. She's doing okay in school. Her grades are good. Not spectacular, but okay. I just assumed it was new material or something." She shook her head, chewing on a thumbnail.

"It must be something. What do we know about this Andy kid? Could it be drugs?"

"Sex, now drugs?" Susan replied, shaking her head adamantly. "Damn, Jason."

"Well, you tell me what it is."

"I don't know." Susan rubbed her face with both hands. "I was thinking the other day about it but didn't want to say anything. I mean, she's taken a liking to wearing black clothes all the time. She's moody, withdrawn. But this…." Susan sighed and looked at her husband. "Do you think it could be about Justin?"

"What?" he asked, sitting up in bed. "No. Surely not. We've been through all this before, Susan. She doesn't even remember him. She was so little."

Susan shrugged. "I don't know. Maybe some kind of repressed memories or something."

Jason shook his head. "I mean, she's eleven. Could she just be getting her period or something?"

Susan rubbed her temples, moaning in frustration. "So every time a female acts weird, it's because of her period?"

"How the hell should I know?" he snapped. "It sure seems to affect you a lot."

"Really, Jason?"

"What?" he asked. "I'm just trying to figure this out too. You don't have to be snotty about it."

Susan rubbed her temples. His idea might not be that far off base, but she wasn't going to let him know that. She made a mental note to ask Miranda about it. Surely, she'd have said something.

Jason put a hand on his wife's leg. "Look,

we've been through all that with the baby."

"He has a name."

Jason took a deep breath, using the time to contain his frustration. "I know he does," he finally said through his teeth. "Anyway, she was three when Justin died. We sent her to doctors and everything. Even they said she wouldn't remember losing a sibling that young. I mean, we only had him for a few months when she was three. She's not shown any signs of remembering him in, what, eight years now?"

"I know what the doctors said, and I know Justin was only four months old, and I know Miranda was only three when he died. I know all of that, Jason. All I'm saying is that there might be some memories that's coming back or something." She looked away, wiping a tear from her cheek.

Jason sighed, softening his stance. "Look, if you think she needs to see Doctor Bellinger again, make an appointment. I don't guess it could hurt anything."

"I want to. I just don't want her to think

that we think something's wrong with her." Susan shook her head.

"Maybe it's a puberty thing. What age do girls have that?"

Susan rolled her eyes. "That's not it."

"Well, I'm out of suggestions. My vote is to make the appointment. If nothing comes of it, fine. If there is something, we'll catch it early." He patted his wife's leg. "Either way, I gotta get some sleep. I've got an early appointment in the morning." He rolled over and pulled the covers up. "Goodnight."

Susan pushed a hand through her hair, clutching her bangs atop her head as she thought. Her eyes drifted to the five-by-seven framed picture on the dresser opposite their bed. It was the only picture they had of her children together. Miranda was sitting in a chair, smiling for the camera, her hair pulled up in pigtails. The baby was more laying across her lap than in her arms, but she'd insisted on holding him. He didn't look happy.

Susan released her hair and wiped another

tear from her cheek. She decided to make the appointment.

Chapter Six

  Miranda's eyes fell on the girl across the waiting room. Like her, she was waiting with her mother. Unlike her, she was rocking gently, twirling a lock of her long blond hair around her index finger. Miranda watched as the curl tightened, drawing the girl's finger next to her scalp. The girl stopped rocking and released the hair, letting it fall to her chest in a bouncy, loose curl. Her hand found another lock of hair and began twirling it. She started rocking again.

  Miranda glanced at her own mother. Like the mother across the room, she was thumbing through an outdated magazine. Did she think

Miranda was as messed up as that girl? Was she as messed up as that girl?

The visit was supposed to be a "routine follow-up," but nothing about it felt routine. Especially since she didn't even remember the first one.

Miranda looked down at her mother's leg, watching as it bounced nervously. Her mother was worried about her. That was both good and bad.

When Susan noticed Miranda staring at her leg, she stopped, offering a smile. Miranda smiled back and then looked away. Out of the corner of her eye, she noticed her mother's leg begin to bounce again.

"Ploughman."

They looked up at the same time, finding a nurse dressed in teal scrubs holding a clipboard. Susan stood. Taking Miranda's hand, she led her to the open doorway.

"The doctor wants to talk to Miranda first. You can wait in here," the nurse told Susan with a smile. She waved her hand at the tiny nook, and the three plastic chairs crowded into it. "Doctor Bellinger will come get you after he's talked with Miranda."

"Oh," Susan said, taken aback slightly. "Okay."

The nurse smiled again. "This is routine, I assure you."

"Yeah. Of course." Susan rubbed Miranda's back. "It'll be okay, sweetie."

Miranda nodded and followed the nurse through the door.

Miranda watched as the tall, thin doctor sat down on the opposite end of the leather couch. He was around her dad's age, but there was a smattering of gray at his temples. Her mother said she'd seen him before, but she didn't remember him. He looked at her, offering a wide, toothy smile.

"So, Miranda, how have you been?"

"I'm good," she replied with a shrug and a half smile.

"School going good?"

"I guess. We've only been back a few weeks."

"Yes, your mom said your grades were good. That's impressive."

Miranda shrugged. "They're okay, I guess." She decided to take a measured approach to his questioning.

"Any new friends?" He turned toward her. Sliding a knee onto the couch, he rested a clipboard on it.

Miranda shrugged as she looked around the office. Her eyes washed across two framed diplomas and a plaque with the doctor's name on it, then fell to the coffee table in front of her. A glass paperweight sat beside a rack of pamphlets. The four leafed clover suspended in the translucent glass was bright green. Written in gold on the leaf were the words, 'It's your lucky day.'

"You like that?" he asked, following her gaze. "My wife gave it to me as a wedding gift."

Miranda nodded. "I like green. It's my favorite color."

"That's nice. I like green too."

"My mom said I've been here before, but I don't remember it."

"You have," he began, nodding. "It was a long time ago. You were young. Plus, we've repainted since then. The walls used to be gray."

Miranda let her eyes wash over the office again, taking in the tan walls. They looked as plain as could be. "I like this color," she lied.

"Me too."

Doctor Bellinger watched Miranda clasp her hands on her lap, then unclasp them. She put an arm on the rest beside her, then clasped her hands together on her lap again. "Are you nervous, Miranda?"

"I don't know. Maybe a little."

"Why are you nervous?"

Miranda shrugged. "I don't know."

"Well, you shouldn't be. I'm not anybody special."

"You're a doctor."

"Do doctors make you nervous?" he asked.

Miranda shrugged again. "Sometimes, if I'm going to get a shot."

"Well, they don't let me give shots, so you're good to go in that department."

"Good, because I don't like getting shots."

"I'm sure nobody does," he said, laughing. When she didn't laugh, he cleared his throat and lifted the clipboard. "Well, let's see here." He perused papers before him. "Your mother is just a little worried about you. New school year and all, I suppose. She just brought you in so we could talk. That's what I do. I just talk to people."

"To see if they're crazy or not?" Miranda asked, watching his face for a reaction. In her mind, she added, Like the girl outside?

"Well, I wouldn't put it that way. Sometimes kids have things that bother them, but they don't exactly know what it is. I help them find out what's bothering them so we can fix it."

"Oh," Miranda replied, nodding. Her

eyes went back to the paperweight. "Nothing's bothering me."

"Are you sure? Your parents are concerned. Can you tell me about the night you stayed out late?"

Miranda shrugged one shoulder casually. "I just fell asleep in the park, is all. I was sitting by a tree, and I fell asleep. When I woke up, it was dark, so I went home."

"Is that all that happened?"

She nodded.

"Was there anyone else with you?"

Miranda shook her head.

"Well, that sounds reasonable enough."

"I told my parents what happened, but I don't think they believed me."

"I'm sure they did. They were probably just worried about you. They love you very much."

Miranda pursed her lips. "I guess so."

"Don't you think they love you?"

"Sometimes they say they do."

"I know them, and I can guarantee you that

they do."

"Some parents don't love their kids."

He nodded sadly. "Unfortunately, that is true in some cases, I guess."

"Why do you think that is?" she asked.

"I couldn't say. I supposed every case is different."

"Am I a 'case'?" she asked.

"I wouldn't say that, exactly." He watched her eyes dart to the window behind him. "You know, Miranda, sometimes the world can be a dangerous place, especially for people your age."

She glanced at him, nodding, then looked back out the window. Turning, he followed her gaze and found a small brown bird perched on the sill outside.

"That's a black-throated sparrow," she informed him.

"Smart girl. Do you like birds, Miranda?"

She nodded, pushing her lips into a pout as she thought. "I guess so. They're useful and pretty. I like the colors some of them have."

"Yes," he agreed. "Some of them are quite beautiful." He jotted down a quick note. "You know, sometimes things happen to those little fellas that they can't help or stop from happening. Some people don't like them and try to hurt them."

Miranda nodded in agreement as she watched the bird. When it flew away, she looked at the doctor. "Nobody's molesting me or anything if that's what you're getting at."

"I didn't say anyone was. I'm just trying to make conversation."

"I know my mother is worried about me for some reason, but nothing's wrong. Nobody's touching my private parts. Nobody's bullying me at school. I'm not on drugs, and I don't have a boyfriend. I'm just a kid. A regular kid." She looked at him and nodded. "And I'm not getting my period."

"Okay," he said, blushing. "Apparently, you're a very bright kid."

Miranda shook her head. "Not really. I'm about as average as you can get, and I'm okay with that."

"Are you really? Okay with things, I mean?"

She nodded emphatically. "I'm good. Honestly."

"Your parents have noticed some changes in your behavior lately. Do you want to talk about that?"

"I'm growing up." She tossed her palms into the air. "Aren't people supposed to change as they get older?"

The doctor laughed. "That they are. Unfortunately, some people never do grow up."

"I'm eleven. I'm growing up. Mystery solved."

"Yes, but it is a tough age." He watched Miranda shrug nonchalantly. "Can I ask you about Justin?" Her eyes widened briefly, then dropped to the floor.

"I guess."

"Do you remember him much?"

"I don't know," she began, toeing the leg of the coffee table. "Sometimes."

"What do you remember, Miranda?"

She shook her head. "Nothing much. I remember seeing him with mom. I remember her feeding him a bottle…maybe. I remember him sleeping a lot. He pooped a lot too."

The doctor chuckled. "That's pretty much all they do at that age."

Miranda looked up at him, then returned her gaze to the floor. "You know, they never talk about him. Not in front of me, at least."

"Maybe they don't want to upset you."

She shrugged. "You'd think they'd say stuff. Sometimes my mother cries. I think it's about him."

"Do you ever cry about him?"

She watched her shoe slide up and down the table leg, her head tilted to one side. "No."

"Why not?"

Her head snapped around. "Why should I?"

"I don't know. He was your baby brother."

"I said I don't remember him much."

"Of course. That sounds reasonable."

He jotted down a note. "Why do you think your parents don't talk about him?"

"I don't know. Grownups do weird stuff."

He chuckled again. "I suppose it seems that way. Anyway, you have lots of other stuff to think about. Right? School. Friends. Grades."

"I guess so."

"Yes, speaking of which, your mother said you've mentioned a new friend." He lifted a page on the clipboard. "Andy, is it?"

Miranda stiffened, then relaxed when she saw him looking at her. She forced a smile and shrugged. "I don't know. He's just a kid that I know. Maybe in my science class. I can't remember."

"Is he a regular kid like you?"

She nodded. "I guess you could say that if you wanted to."

"So Andy is a real boy?"

Miranda's brow furrowed. "He's real."

"Is Andy your new boyfriend?"

"What?" she asked, shocked. "Definitely not. He's just some kid."

"What do you and Andy do together?"

"Nothing, really. Just talk."

"Why don't you bring your friend to your parents for supper or just to play?"

"I don't think he'd like that. Besides, my house is…."

"Is what?" he asked.

Miranda shrugged. "Sad, I guess."

"Because Justin died?"

"Why else?"

The doctor nodded. He decided not to push too hard but made a note to talk about Justin more on her next visit. "So let me make sure I have everything. School is fine. Your parents are weird. Nobody's messing with you. No bullies are bullying you. You're incredibly average and happy with that, and Andy is just some random kid that might or might not be in your science class. Is that all?"

Miranda shrugged, a smile tugging at the corners of her mouth. "Sounds just like my life."

"Well, that didn't take long." He looked at

his watch. "Fifteen minutes. That's a record." He paused, rubbing his chin. "But your folks paid for an hour. What are we going to do for a half hour or so?"

"I don't know," she said with a shrug. "You could take a nap or maybe order a pizza."

"Both are excellent ideas, but I've already had lunch, and if I take a nap, I won't sleep well tonight."

"You got any board games?"

He laughed. "No, but I really should get some."

"There's computer games. You have a computer, don't you?"

"I do, but there's only solitaire on it. You'd find it boring, I'm sure."

"Any games on your phone?"

"Nope. Sorry."

"Your job sounds boring."

He laughed again. "Some days it is, to be perfectly honest. But some days, you get to meet nice people like you, and it's not so bad." Miranda nodded, her eyes darting past him to the window. He watched her eyes narrow. Her body tensed slightly, and she didn't know what to do with her hands again.

He turned to the window and found a large black bird staring at them through the glass. The bird itself was perfectly still, but its dark eye darted back and forth between them.

"It's like it can see us," Miranda whispered.

"I don't think so. There's probably a glare on the glass. He probably sees himself and thinks it's another bird."

Miranda shook her head. "They're smarter than that." She tilted her head far to the right, and the bird mimicked her movements. "Ravens are some of the smartest birds there is."

"That's interesting." The doctor shifted his position, and the bird's eye darted to him. He cleared his throat loudly, hoping to scare it away. "Is it a crow or a raven?"

"It's a raven. Their tails are different. Plus, ravens are bigger than crows. Smarter too. Experts think they can count as high as four."

"Uh huh," he said, bending forward to get a better look at the bird. The matte blackness of the feathers looked out of place in the sunshine on his windowsill. It was more like a void than anything else, an absence. He stared into the dark eye, watching the bird watch him. He'd never seen one this close. They were bigger than expected.

"A flock of crows is called a murder."

"I've heard that," he said absently, lost in the bird's gaze.

"Know what a flock of ravens is called?"

"I haven't the faintest idea," he said, still watching the bird.

"An unkindness. Isn't that the oddest thing?"

"An unkindness?" he asked, sparing her a quick glance before turning back to the window. "That does sound odd."

"In the old days, people believed that a raven represented a secret. It was said that if you have a secret, a raven will show up. Do you have a secret, Doctor?"

"Uh huh," he said absently, still watching the bird. He looked at Miranda, puzzled. "The more pertinent question might be if you have a secret, Miranda?"

"Doesn't everybody?" she asked with a one sided smile.

A hollow chuckle escaped the doctor as he looked back to the bird, watching its dark eye dart around the room.

"Can they keep a secret?" he asked, nodding to the raven outside.

"Apparently not," she said flatly, her eyes now locked on the raven.

"What does that mean?"

"Nothing," she replied flatly.

Miranda watched him turn back to the raven. "Did you know that if allowed to, they will eat the body of a dead human and not even think twice about it? Maybe that's why a group of them is called that. An unkindness."

Doctor Bellinger shook his head, snatched

from his trance by her words. "That's a rather morbid thought, Miranda," he said, standing. "Okay, mister raven crow, whatever you are, it's time for you to go." He went to the window and waved his hands at the bird. It hopped to the other end of the sill but didn't fly away. Looking up at him, it let out a loud, defiant squawk.

Doctor Bellinger looked over his shoulder at Miranda, finding her watching intently. He forced a laugh to bring some levity to the strange uneasiness of the situation. "Persistent little bugger, isn't he?"

"Don't open the window, Doctor. He'll peck your eyes out. I know he will." Miranda's voice was stoic, distant.

"I don't think it's all that," he waved his hands at the window again, but still, the bird remained. "The dentist next door has a bird feeder. This guy's probably just looking for an easy meal."

"Ravens are opportunistic feeders."

He looked back at Miranda. She was staring at the bird, but her hands had gripped the hem of her tee shirt, kneading the fabric with her fingertips. Her lips were pursed tightly; her brow creased by deep lines. There was a pall about her face that hadn't been there before. Her entire complexion had changed.

"Are you okay, Miranda?" he asked, stepping away from the widow.

Outside, the raven released a series of low croaks. The doctor spun, opening its line of sight to Miranda. The bird hopped closer to the window, turning its head to the side so that the dark eye faced directly at her. The bird pushed closer to the glass, its unblinking stare fixed on Miranda.

"It can see me," she said quietly.

"Miranda, It's just a bird, a crow. That's all it is. No need to be upset."

"That's what they do. They sit and watch you, figure you out. They're always there, studying us. Waiting."

"Miranda, please. It's just a dumb bird."

"Oh, they're not dumb at all, but you do have to show them who's boss." In one smooth motion, Miranda sprang from the couch, grabbed the paperweight from the table and hurled it at the window. It sailed past the doctor and struck the glass directly in line with the crow's neck. The inner pane shattered, sending a shower of glass onto the carpet.

The doctor gasped, watching the glass ball fall to the floor and wobble towards him. It came to a stop in front of his right shoe, the words "It's your lucky day" staring up at him.

"Okay," he said, going quickly to Miranda. "That's enough. Time to get your mother." He put an arm around her shoulders and buzzed the nurse with his free hand. Looking back to the window, he saw the bird looking at them through the spider web of cracks. Its dark eye was frozen in a stare directly at Miranda.

The raven let out a loud squawk that filled the office, then turned and waddled to the edge of the sill. It spared them one last glance, then flew away.

When his receptionist answered, he said,

"Send in Mrs. Ploughman." He shook his head, his eyes pulled back to the window. Pressing the call button again, he added, "Quickly."

"Why, Miranda? Do you even know the implications of what you've done?" Jason Ploughman stared down at his daughter. Her tears broke his heart, but the echoes of his wife's panicked voice were still ringing through his mind.

"I'm sorry. I didn't mean to."

"You didn't mean to pick up a paperweight and throw it through a window?" He stomped across Miranda's bedroom and back to her. "You just accidentally threw it?"

"No," she sobbed. "That's not it."

Jason rubbed his forehead, sighing. "Look, Miranda, you've gotta talk to me because you're in a world of crap right now."

"I know." Miranda wiped her cheeks with the heels of her hands. "Dad, please, don't yell anymore. I'm sorry. I'll pay for the window out of my allowance."

Jason's shoulders slumped, his resolve weakening. He sat on the edge of her bed and pulled her hands from her face. "It's not about the window, Miranda. What. Happened?"

"I don't know. I mean...." she trailed off, shaking her head.

"Baby, 'I don't know' isn't going to cut it." He cradled her cheek in his hand. "Tell me why you did it."

"I don't— I can't really explain it. We were talking. Everything was fine, and then this raven landed on the windowsill. It was just staring at us. We were talking about it, but the doctor started acting weird. He went to the window and tried to shoo it away, but it wouldn't leave. He was getting mad, or scared, or something. I don't know. He kept trying to get rid of it, but it kept looking at us. He was upset. I just wanted it to go away. I'm sorry, Daddy." She fell into his chest, sobbing.

"What do you mean he was acting weird?"

"He was nervous about it. I think he didn't want it looking at him or something. He kept waving his hands around, telling it to go away. I just kinda reacted. I don't know why. I really am sorry."

Jason stroked his daughter's hair, holding her to him. When he'd entered her room, he was sure Miranda was at fault. Now he wondered if the doctor shared in some of it. He was the adult, a professional no less.

Miranda sat halfway down the staircase, listening to her parents talk about her. Their voices floated to her from the kitchen. They'd talked late into the night and picked up where they left off over breakfast. Things were bad. Worse than she thought.

"She said he was acting weird, Susan. Why would she say it if he wasn't?"

"For the tenth time. I. Don't. Know."

"There's a tape or something, isn't there? I mean, don't they tape the sessions with kids? Maybe we can watch it."

"I'm not going to ask him for that. It makes it sound like we think he did something wrong."

"If he didn't," her father insisted, "Then he shouldn't have a problem letting us see the tape."

Miranda chewed her thumbnail during a short silence.

"Look," her father said, "This is our daughter we're talking about. We deserve to know the facts. All the facts. I want to see the tape. I'll call him if you want. I don't mind if he gets his feelings hurt."

"No," Susan insisted. "Jason, no. I'll call him and see if he can email it over or something. I don't want you barging up in there like a raging bull accusing him of something."

"I'm not accusing anybody of anything. Miranda said she was reacting to the way he was acting. I mean, damn, Susan. Don't you think this is out of character for her? Even with everything going on lately?"

"I'm not saying that it didn't."

"Then what are you saying? He's already

talking about medicines and behavior therapy. My God, he makes it sound like she's off her rocker. You don't treat prepubescence with Thorazine, Susan."

"Something's wrong, Jason. I can feel it. I don't know what it is, but I just have this gut feeling."

"Not to dismiss your gut, but I want to see the tape. I have one meeting just before lunch that couldn't be moved. I have to make it. See if he can send it over this afternoon."

The clink of dishes being placed in the sink warned Miranda that they were done. She stood and hurried back up the stairs in socked feet. Climbing back into bed, she pulled the covers to her chin. Everything was going wrong. She didn't get to visit Andy yesterday at all, and today wasn't looking any better. She'd messed everything up. Everything. Now she'd probably never be able to see him again.

Miranda clenched her eyes, pushing a tear down her cheek. She couldn't just leave him there, alone. She just couldn't. She wouldn't. He needed her. What if the ravens came back? What if something pulled the tarp away?

She covered her mouth with her hands and looked at the door to her bedroom. She couldn't tell them about Andy. They wouldn't understand even if she tried to explain. They'd take him away, and she'd never see him again.

Ain't he a dandy? Dandy Andy.

Miranda shook her head to make the voice go away.

She'd promised him everything would be okay.

He needed her.

He did.

Chapter Seven

"You ready?" Susan asked. Jason's meeting had stretched into the afternoon, and after running errands, it was after three when he got home. "Doctor Bellinger said there's no sound. Something about HIPPA laws."

When her husband shrugged, she hit play on the laptop on the desk in front of her. The computer screen showed the inside of Doctor Bellinger's office. Miranda was on one end of a couch. The doctor was on the other.

"Looks normal enough."

Susan chewed on a thumbnail as she

watched her daughter interact with the doctor. Her husband was right. It looked like a normal conversation. Until the bird showed up on the windowsill.

"What are they looking at?" Jason asked, leaning closer to the screen. "Is it a crow?"

"Doctor Bellinger said they were discussing Justin, then the bird showed up. That's when he said things started going south."

"Look at him," Jason said, watching the video of the doctor waving his hands at the window. "Miranda said he was acting weird."

"He said that she seemed uncomfortable that it was there. He was just trying to make it fly off."

"Doesn't seem to be working. Mister crow ain't scared."

Susan nodded. "Miranda said it was a raven."

"What's the difference?"

Susan shrugged. "The doctor said she was insistent that it was a raven, and that she was saying something about 'unkindness' or something."

"An unkindness of ravens?"

"Yeah. That's it? What is that?"

"A flock of ravens is called an unkindness."

She looked at him, surprised. "How the hell do you know that?"

Jason shrugged. "Just one of those random things that sticks in your head, I guess. Like, a flock of crows is called a murder. A pride of lions. A flock of seagulls."

Susan stared at him for a moment, then shook her head. She turned back to the screen just in time to see Miranda grab the paperweight and hurl it at the window.

"Look at her face. She looks scared."

"A little ticked off too." Jason stood with a sigh. "It was a hell of a throw, though. Did you see it? If the window weren't there, she'd have killed that sucker," he said, a proud smile on his face.

"That's what you're taking from all this? Our daughter freaks out in a psychiatrist's office, and you're happy she's got a good arm?"

"I don't know. She could have freaked out a psychiatrist and missed." He absorbed his wife's glare and shrugged. "Anyway, Miranda was right. He was acting a little weird. Did you see him staring at it like that?"

"Still...." Susan rubbed her face with both hands. "What are we going to do?"

Jason shrugged again. "Find a new shrink?"

"I'm serious. With all that's been going on, you can't deny that something's bothering her."

"Maybe it's just a rough patch. Hell, I don't know."

"I'm worried, Jason."

"Look," he began, putting his hands on Susan's shoulders as he moved behind her. "It's going to be okay."

"I don't know. I'm just so worried."

"That's understandable," he said, massaging her shoulders.

Susan shook her head as she closed the screen. The computer reverted to the last open video, showing Susan's mother holding Justin. She was standing in their kitchen, bouncing him in her arms while Miranda doddered about at her feet.

Jason winced as her high-pitched voice came through the speakers.

"Just look at those cheeks," she said. "I could just eat him up." Virginia Ainsworth turned, carefully avoiding Miranda. "Just look at him, ain't he a dandy?"

"Andy!" Miranda exclaimed at her feet, her hands stretching up for the baby. "Andy. Andy."

"Your mother," Jason said with a smirk. "Her voice kills me."

"Stop," Susan said, looking at her son. "Look at our sweet baby. He was so beautiful."

Jason hugged her from behind. "C'mon, babe. Don't do this again. Stop torturing yourself."

"I'm okay," she said, patting his hand. "I just miss him so bad sometimes."

Jason looked at the image of his son and smiled. "I know," he said with a sigh. His eyes drifted down to the three year old Miranda, urgently tugging on her grandmother's pants leg.

"Andy, Andy," the young Miranda chirped.

"Why is she saying that?" he asked.

"It's my mother. She was saying, 'He's a dandy,' talking about Justin. Miranda couldn't say 'dandy,' I guess." Susan's brow furrowed as she watched her daughter stumble around, arms outstretched toward the baby.

She shook her head as a pang of guilt struck her. Removed from the chaos of the moment, she began to realize how Miranda could feel neglected, forgotten. New babies were fun, exciting but also demanding.

"Honestly," she said, "I never noticed it before." A hand went to her mouth as she watched her daughter vie for attention.

"What does that even mean, 'He's a dandy'?"

"Who knows?" Susan asked. "Have you met my mother?"

"Yes," he said with a laugh. "Unfortunately, I have."

Jason Ploughman found his wife on the couch in the den. It had been a strained evening, and though it was barely dark outside, she'd already fallen asleep. He sighed and went to her, taking the blanket from the back of the couch and covering her with it. He then collected the empty wine bottle and glass from the end table and switched the light off as he left the room.

Upstairs, he checked on Miranda, finding her tucked into bed as well, fast asleep. A pained smile slid across his lips. Despite the uproar surrounding her lately, she was a good kid. "Goodnight, kiddo. Sleep tight." He sighed, watching her sleep. She looked so peaceful, practically angelic.

It's just a rough patch, he told himself. She's going to be fine. He backed out of the room, closing the door behind him. He started down the hall but stopped at the door next to Miranda's bedroom. A hand went to the knob, but he didn't turn it. Beyond the door was Justin's nursery, just as it had been the day they'd found him dead in his crib.

Jason closed his eyes, his free hand covering his mouth. Opening his eyes, he stared at the door. He couldn't do it. He couldn't go in. Susan did sometimes, he knew. But he couldn't. He released the knob with a sigh and walked down the hall to his own bedroom, closing the door behind him. When the sound of her parent's door closing filtered into her room, Miranda opened her eyes. She laid still for a while longer, watching her own door. When it didn't open after five minutes, she threw the covers back. Dressed in a pair of jeans and a long-sleeved tee shirt, she threw her legs over the edge of the bed and stood. She slipped her feet into a pair of shoes and went to the window. After crawling out, she reached back inside and grabbed her backpack, hauling it out the window. She shimmied across the roof of their front porch and dropped the pack. Lying on her belly, she shimmied over the edge and dropped onto the soft carpet of grass. Kneeling in the shadows, she waited to see if anyone had seen her. Sure that the coast was clear, she slipped the pack on, and hurried across the yard, slipped through the wooden fence, and disappeared into the woods.

"Hello, Andy," Miranda said, working her way down the gentle slope toward him. "I'm sorry I couldn't come yesterday. Things are complicated at my house." She scanned the mound of leaves with the flashlight. There were a few divots, but nothing big had been here. That was good. If her worst fears had been true, she wouldn't have been able to forgive herself.

Andy was okay.

"I might stay a while if that's okay with you," she said with a smile, dropping the pack. "I brought some stuff to read." She pulled a library book from the pack. "It's got stories about pirates and stuff like that. Not my thing, but I thought you'd like it better than the last one." She'd spent most of the summer reading aloud from a book about a girl made of glass. The ending had upset Andy, but she thought it was probably the best way to end such a peculiar tale.

She held the new book up to the mound, then laid it atop the leaves next to the stuffed lion. "Oh, and I brought more candles. I know you like them."

A strained smile came to her lips as she looked at the mound of leaves in front of her. She drew in a hitchy breath, tracing the underneath of the lean-to shelter with the light. Turning, she moved the beam around the clearing, pausing on the body of each raven.

When she was done, she sighed, her shoulders drooping. "My parents think I'm nuts." She shook her head. "They wouldn't understand." She slid a hand over the lens of the flashlight, smiling absently as the light shined through them, turning her skin a bright red.

"And that stupid doctor. Ugh!" She dug a

candle out of the pack stashed beneath the leaves. "He's some kind of head-shrinker or something. That's what my dad called him, I think." She lit two of the candles and sat them on the flat rock between her and Andy.

"One of the ravens came while I was there. I'm sure it was one of these." She cast her eyes to the darkened sky. "The doctor tried to say it was a crow, but I told him it wasn't. He wouldn't listen, though. Grownups never listen to us kids, even if it's their job to."

Miranda pushed her pack toward Andy's head and laid down on it, facing the lean-to. "I think they're going to send me away or something. I saw this girl in the waiting room. She looked really messed up." She stared at the candle's flame for a moment. "I wonder what happened to her to make her go nuts?"

She shifted her gaze to Andy, nodding. "Yeah, maybe she was born that way." She rolled onto her back. The opening in the canopy afforded her a sliver of the night sky. Her eyes scanned the stars, wondering what her parents would do when they got up, and she wasn't there. Would they search for her, or just not care, like Andy's parents?

"Do you think things happen for a reason, Andy?" she asked thoughtfully. "I mean, like, I don't think I just randomly found you." She smiled, sparing Andy a glance. "That's sweet. I'm glad I found you too. But don't you think this was meant to be? I mean, Mister Blabbermouth over there—" she looked toward the raven whose mouth she'd bound. The bird was just visible in the soft glow of the candles. "—did lead me to you."

She pushed herself up onto an elbow and looked at Andy. "I wish I'd met you before…you know." She nodded solemnly. "Maybe I could have helped somehow." She laid back down, bending her arm around the top of her head and wondered again how Andy died. It was nothing as wild as a gunshot or even being beaten to death. He probably wasn't strangled, either. That left marks. She wanted to ask but thought it impertinent. Kids died. Did it really matter how they died?

It does to the cops. And to their parents.

Miranda winced as her head erupted with a loud, guttural caw. She spun around, wide-eyed, with the flashlight in her hand. The beam fell on the raven directly behind her. Her eyes narrowed as she stared at it.

"What do you want?" She stood and crossed the clearing, keeping the bird centered in the beam of light. It hung just above eye level, its wings spread wide by a small limb. It stared back at her with eyeless sockets, its dark beak opened in a perpetual scream. "You don't know anything about my little brother! You're just a stupid bird.

"Next time you think you have something smart to say, just remember who put you on that tree." She jabbed the flashlight at its breast. When the feathers began to move, she stepped back with a gasp. Her eyes bulged, and she took another cautious step back, watching the abdomen undulate.

When it went still, she reclaimed a step, bending forward to examine the bird. Its wings were still tied to the stick, holding them outstretched. Its legs and feet hung stiffly in front of a ragged tail. The nail she'd driven through its neck still protruded, half bent, from the black feathers. The stick she'd used to hold its head up was clearly visible. It was still dead.

Dead is dead.

Ain't he a dandy?

Miranda shook her head to silence the high-pitched voice, which to her, was beginning to take on the tone of a crow's caw.

Scanning the ground with the light, she found a good stick. She poked the bird's abdomen with it, gasping again as it began to move. Her eyes narrowed as she stepped closer. What started as fear grew into indignation, but that was quickly turning to anger. Something was in there. Something was inside the raven's chest cavity. Her raven.

She raised the stick, a thin smile coming to her lips. She struck the bird's abdomen hard enough to loosen a handful of feathers. They erupted from it and floated to the ground like confetti. From inside the raven, something let out a high-pitched squeal. She hit the bird again, harder. More feathers flew into the air, revealing the dry skin beneath. The whole bird shook, the high-pitched squeal continuous now.

She hit the bird again, and the skin erupted, spilling a wounded rat and her babies onto the ground. The rat tried to escape, dragging the guts hanging from its ruptured stomach. Miranda moved quickly, delivering three rapid blows with the stick that silenced the squeals.

Pursing her lips, she found each of the four pink bodies scattered beneath the raven. One by one, she went to them, delivering an emphatic stomp on each. When she was done, she looked around.

"Anybody else have something to say?" She spun quickly, centering the raven closest to Andy in the beam. One of the earliest ones, its body badly decayed. Most of the feathers were gone from the tail, and its outstretched wings resembled an upside down picket fence.

"Look at you," she said, stomping up to it. "You're supposed to be guarding Andy and warning the others to stay away." She shook her head. "You're pitiful." She hit it across the breast with the stick, watching with disgust as the legs and a chunk of the lower abdomen fell to the ground.

She turned from it with an exasperated sigh. "What about you?" She asked, going to another bird, a relative newcomer. Its black feathers shined in the flashlight's beam. She gave the bird a whack with the stick, but it remained intact.

"Very well," she said with a curt nod. She walked past the raven, then spun and delivered a sweeping blow. There was a soft crack as the ribcage collapsed. Three feathers slipped free and gently floated to the ground. "I should have known."

She closed her eyes, panting through clenched teeth as her fist tightened around the stick. "I can't trust any of you. You're all useless!" She lashed out, striking the bird again. The blow landed alongside the raven's neck, breaking the stick inside its throat. The head fell forward, hanging limply against what was left of its chest.

She grunted and swung again. More feathers flew, and rage erupted in her eyes. She ran across the clearing and struck a different bird. Its chest burst open, sending feathers in every direction. Miranda growled through clenched teeth, hitting it repeatedly. She ran from bird to bird, whipping them mercilessly with the stick until the ground and the air were thick with the smell of rot and black feathers.

Lost in her frustration and anger, she closed her eyes and threw her face skyward. Turning slowly, she stretched out her arms, dropping the stick and the light. A low guttural cry began in her throat but quickly grew into a scream. Feathers drifted gently down upon her face like snowflakes while others landed, quill first, in her hair.

Fingertips went to her cheek and found a feather. A smile came to her lips as she drug the tip of it across her skin. She groped blindly at the air, catching more feathers as they drifted in the air. Clutching them in her fingertips, she formed a narrow fan, like a raven's tail. Dragging them down her face, she let them gently brush over her lips as her smile grew.

Her eyes opened suddenly, and she laughed. Her voice rang out through the empty forest loud and clear. In the distance, a raven answered noisily, awakening other members of the unkindness. Within seconds, the tree they'd roosted in was amuck with their calls. Seconds later, the entire flock erupted into the night sky.

Chapter Eight

"What do you mean she's gone?" Jason Ploughman asked, pushing past his wife and rushing to Miranda's room. He snatched the covers from her bed, then went to the closet and threw the door open. He checked the bathroom, then stood in the center of the room with his hands on his hips.

"I knew it. I just knew something was wrong," Susan moaned, pushing her hands through her hair. "Should we call the cops? We should call the cops."

"Have you searched the house?"

"No, I haven't searched the house, but I haven't seen her all morning. That's why I came to check on her."

Jason covered his face with both hands, sighing through them. "Where would she go?"

"I don't know, Jason. We should call the police."

"Call her friends. You know them, don't you, or their parents?"

"I know some of the parents." Susan turned and hurried down the steps, muttering that they should call the police.

Susan ended the call, shaking her head as she dropped the cell phone on the kitchen table.

Jason sighed. "Maybe we should drive around again. Where was she the other day? The park?"

"Yes. That's what she said."

"Which park?" Jason asked.

"I don't know. I assumed the one down on Bradberry. It's between here and the school."

"I'll go search there. You stay here in case someone calls."

Susan nodded absently, her grasp on control waning. "I knew something was wrong," she said, melting into a kitchen chair. "I knew it."

Miranda tossed the small metal cup aside, the tea candle spent. It landed on the pile just past the end of the lean-to. The night had consumed more candles than she'd expected, but it was worth it.

She held up the windbreaker, surveying the night's work. By poking tiny holes in the fabric and using melted wax to hold them in place, she'd attached the loose feathers from the ravens to the jacket. Their oily black sheen stared back at her in the morning light. The feathers covered the body of the jacket in smooth, even rows. The shorter feathers of the body did well on the sleeves and filling in gaps.

She stood and put it on, sparing a glance at the bodies of the ravens she'd nailed to the trees. They hung featherless, many of them mere skeletons, staring back at her accusingly. She pulled the jacket closed and strode back and forth in front of the lean-to.

"What do you think, Andy?" she asked. "Do you like it?" Miranda laughed, throwing a hand toward the mound of leaves. "Oh, you're too kind." Looking down at the jacket, she smiled. "You're right. It is perfect." Her hands slid down the front, her fingers dancing along the feathers. It's absolutely perfect."

Her head jerked up suddenly, her smile fading. She stared at the mound of leaves that covered Andy's body and nodded. "You're right. They will come looking for me now that it's light." Her fingers toyed with the feathers as she thought. "They'll come looking for me, and they'll find you."

After a short pause, she nodded and said, "I know. They want to send me away and take you somewhere. I'll never see you again." She fell to the ground next to the mound, patting the lion gently. "It's okay. I won't let them take you away. I promise."

Miranda looked up, her eyes searching the woods in front of her. Finally, she looked back at the mound. "Now that's an idea." She nodded. "I think it just might work too." She smiled. "You're such a smart boy, Andy."

Miranda's head twitched violently as the voice echoed through her mind once again.

Ain't he a dandy?

Chilled by the night, the creek was cold, but Miranda barely noticed. She grabbed a handful of the dark mud and ripped it from beneath the water. Lathering it between her hands, she quickly spread it over her hands and wrists. When she was done, she gathered more and closed her eyes. Bringing her hand to her face, she pushed the mud across her cheeks, then spread it across the rest of her face and neck, covering her skin in a black mask.

As the pool settled, she stared at her reflection on the surface. Her face was covered in a film of dark mud, leaving only her sandy brown hair and a pair of green eyes that stared back at her. Almost everything about her was gone now. Almost.

They don't understand, she thought. They'll never understand.

She plunged both hands into the water with an angry grunt. Bringing forth two fists full of mud, she raised them to her head, hesitated, then began smearing the mud over her hair. Working slowly, she massaged the mud with her fingers before gathering the length at the nape of her neck. She pulled it through her hands, making sure to coat the entire length.

When she was done, she ran both hands over her hair to smooth it, and her eyes dropped again to the reflection on the water. The girl staring back at her was someone different now. Nodding, a smile crept to her lips. Nothing was left now. The voices were quiet. The memories were gone. Now she could be the girl she was meant to be. And she had work to do.

Perched on the edge of the couch in an exhausted doze, Susan jumped when the phone in her hand began to buzz. Cursing, she grabbed the phone from the floor between her feet and looked at it. The alert was finally going out.

ALERT! ALERT! ALERT! MISSING CHILD
Possible runaway/possible abduction
Miranda June Ploughman Age, 11
Height: 4 ft. 8 in. Weight, 80 lbs.
Black hair, Green eyes.
Last seen 4209 James Avenue
Contact your local law enforcement
with any information or call 911.

Susan stared dumbly at the alert on her phone. Was Miranda that tall, she wondered? She was tall for a girl. It was possible. Her side of the family was all tall.

"Hey, baby." The voice was high pitched, the southern accent thick.

Susan looked up and found her mother standing in the doorway to the den. She, too, was holding her phone.

"How you holding up?"

Susan looked from her mother to her phone then back to her mother. She held the phone up, showing her the alert and burst into sobs. Seeing the alert drove home the truth that her child was missing. Not at a friend's house, not just late coming home, but missing.

Gone.

Victoria Ainsworth rushed across the room and wrapped her daughter in her arms. "It'll be okay, sweetheart. I know it will."

Susan shook her head. "No, it won't, Mama. I've got a feeling that it won't."

Virginia pulled her daughter's head to her chest, shushing her. "Don't talk like that. I've called all the women at church. They'll be praying around the clock. They'll find her, baby. They'll find our little girl." She closed her eyes, saying another prayer. Her daughter had lost one child already. Surely, she wouldn't have to suffer the loss of another.

Miranda squatted on her bare feet, her arms wrapped around her knees, and watched the ridge on the other side of the hollow. Just as she'd thought they would, the police had begun to search the woods. At first, they'd only checked the edges behind her house, but as the day stretched into the afternoon, they'd pushed deeper. They were still far away from Andy, but if they were serious and knew where to look, they could find him within the hour.

She shrugged her windbreaker up on her

shoulders despite the warmth of the day. The feathers afforded her a good camouflage, and she liked wearing it. She nuzzled her cheek against the feathers on her shoulder, and the briefest of smiles tugged at the corners of her mouth.

The group was just beyond the other ridge. There were a lot of them, and they weren't trying to be quiet. When a blue baseball cap appeared over the top of the hill, her eyes darted to it. Soon there were five others. Four men and two women milled about atop the ridge. One of them pulled out a pair of binoculars and scanned the hollow between her and them.

Miranda didn't move. The man with the binoculars might be able to differentiate her from the bush she was hiding behind, but he wasn't looking at her. She smiled when one of the women stopped and bent over. She used her phone to take a picture of something on the ground, then began typing on it. When she was done, she called out to the group.

The searchers gathered around her, looking

at the ground. Finally, one of the men bent and picked it up. He examined it carefully, then showed one of the other men. A quiet mumble of voices lofted gently to her, then one of the men took out his radio.

Of course they'd found the candy wrapper. She wanted them to find it. If they weren't dumb, they'd also find the path that she'd cleared by dragging her feet through the leaves. If they followed it, they'd head off in a direction that would take them away from Andy.

Another smile tried to come to her lips when the group fanned out again and started walking away from her. She'd make the same trip this morning, leaving clues that would take them far from here. She sat motionless, moving nothing but her eyes, and watched the group disappear amongst the trees.

Finally, she sighed and stood slowly, keeping an eye out for the search party. Their voices lingered in the forest after they'd moved beyond her sight. She waited until the voices faded to a whisper, then turned and headed back to Andy.

They were safe, for now.

Virginia Ainsworth looked up from the scrap of well-worn purple cloth clutched in her hands. Seconds after the back door opened and closed, her son-in-law appeared in the kitchen. He stopped suddenly when he saw her, then moved to the cabinet in the corner.

"Anything?" she asked, hopefully.

"No sign of her," he said, pulling down a bottle of scotch and a crystal tumbler. He poured himself a drink and downed it, then poured another. "One of the teams found a candy wrapper," he added, going to the fridge to get some ice. "But I don't know."

"What kind of candy?"

He stared at her for a moment, then his face softened. Although he wasn't her biggest fan, the woman was obviously worried sick about his daughter. "A Payday."

"That's Miranda's favorite," she said, nodding.

He agreed with her. "They followed what they thought might have been a trail and found some other stuff. A place where it looked like someone sat down for a while. A couple miles away, they found a scrap of black fabric on a broken branch. And a feather."

"A feather?" Virginia asked.

He nodded. "A black feather, like from a crow or something."

"What does it mean?"

Jason shrugged. "I don't know. Maybe nothing. Someone said it was a good sign, that crows were inquisitive. Like maybe if she were there, they'd be curious and check her out."

"That's encouraging."

"We're grasping at straws now." Jason sipped his drink then shook his head. "They called me, and I hauled ass over there. We searched for miles but didn't find anything else. We had to stop because it got too dark. One of the volunteers rolled an ankle coming out." He sighed, staring at the wall.

"They'll find her. I just know they will."

He nodded. "I hope so." A hand rubbed his forehead, "Where's Susan?"

"The doctor sent her over some valium. She took one about an hour ago and fell asleep on the couch in the den."

Jason took another sip of his drink, grimacing as it went down.

"Susan said that maybe Miranda was upset."

Jason shrugged. "I don't know."

"She said it might be about the baby, about Justin."

"I don't know, Virginia. Maybe, maybe not. There's just no way to tell."

She gripped the cloth in her fist. "Do you think she blames herself?"

"What?" he asked, shocked. "Why would you ask that?"

"I don't know. You always hear that when couples get divorced, the kids think it's their fault.

Kid's minds don't work like ours do. There's no telling what's going on inside her little head, you know."

"That's probably true," he sighed, "But I don't see how it could be about Justin. It's been years, Virginia. Why now? Why not back then?" He shook his head. "It doesn't make any sense. I don't think that's it."

"Okay," she said, not wanting to be a nuisance. "Look, you're tired and dirty. Take a hot shower and get some rest. I'll stay up all night by the phones."

Jason finished his drink and looked at the glass, considering another one. It would help, he knew, but he also needed to be ready to go on a moment's notice. He finally sat the glass down on the counter and started around the table. Virginia grabbed his arm, stopping him.

"Jason, look, I know you're not just thrilled with me, and I'm sorry if I've been an imposition over the years."

"Virginia," he sighed tiredly. "You're my

wife's mother, grandmother to my child, and I know you love them both. Ultimately, what I think doesn't matter one damned bit. I appreciate you for looking after Susan."

The older woman smiled. "I've been praying for you, too," she said, showing him the cloth clutched in her other hand. "We all have."

His eyes went to the cloth, then to her face. "Do me a favor, okay? Tell everyone to stop praying for me, or for Susan for that matter, and focus your attention on finding Miranda alive and well. Okay?"

"There's enough praying for the lot of you."

He smiled. "Well, Virginia, I sure as hell hope so."

Miranda sat on the ground with her legs crossed. The jacket that she'd created was draped over her shoulders. Her elbows were on her knees, propping her fists beneath her chin. Much of the mud had dried and flaked off, leaving patches of skin dyed gray by the pigments. It was okay, though. She'd get more in the morning.

She stared at the small tea candles burning on the flat rock between her and Andy. The woods had gone quiet with the coming night, but they'd gotten darker and more frightful as well. So much so that she'd decided to light a second candle. They could scarcely afford the luxury, but the light was reassuring.

"It's really blown up now, you know," she muttered. "There's cops and volunteers and just all sorts of people." Miranda shook her head. "It's just so unfair. Nobody did all of this when you...." she hated to mention that Andy was dead. Of course they both knew he was but coming out and saying it felt rude. "When I found you. Nobody was searching for you."

She looked up, her eyes scanning the shadows in front of her. "I guess so," she sighed. "Your folks didn't call the cops. I'm so sorry, Andy. You deserved so much better."

She picked up a leaf and held a tip over the candle. The dry material caught instantly. Fire crackled and danced across the face of the leaf, for a moment leaving a skeleton of the inner structure. Miranda watched it burn, then dropped it onto the rock before fetching another.

"You know, this isn't the first time there's been a big blow-up at my house." She lit another leaf, turning it slowly as it burned, her eyes locked on the flames. "I used to have a little brother named Justin." She twirled the burned stem in her fingers, staring at its charred remains. "But he died."

Miranda picked up another leaf. "I was little, but I remember him. Then one day, he was just gone. My folks just started acting like he never existed. There's only one picture of him in our whole house." She held another leaf over the flame and watched it catch fire. Raising it to eye level, her eyes narrowed, following the flame's march across it. "Isn't that weird? I mean, just one picture. It's in my parents' bedroom, and it's not very big." She traced the slender trail of smoke as it rose into the air, following it until it disappeared into the darkness.

She shrugged. "Maybe so. Who knows why parents do the things they do?" She twirled the leaf slowly as it finished burning. Her eyes glassed over as she faded back into the memory. "I was the first one who knew. My parents were still asleep. I woke up early and wanted to see the baby, so I went into the nursery." Miranda closed her eyes, reliving the day. "He was so little."

Her head jerked as a voice echoed through it.

Ain't he a dandy?

Miranda squinted as she watched the ember on the end of the stem move slowly toward her fingertips. "I wanted to play with him, but he was asleep." The glowing ember moved closer to her fingers. A tiny plume of smoke danced in her voice as she spoke. "I called him, but he didn't wake up. I reached through the bars and shook him. He still didn't wake up."

She pinched the end of the stem as the

ember moved closer. "I never told anybody, but I found him first. He was cold." She shook her head. "His little hands were like ice. His fingertips were blue. I thought they were pretty, like someone had painted them."

The ember continued its slow march to her fingertips. The ember met her skin, but she held it tight. The faint smell of burning flesh rose into the air, the pain made her hand shake. She held the stem until the ember finally faded.

Dropping the stem, she looked at the tiny black dots on the end of her thumb and forefinger. She spit on then, then rubbed it on her pants leg.

"What did I do?" she asked, looking up at Andy. She shook her head. "Nothing." She nodded. "Yep. My baby brother died, and I didn't even cry. I didn't do anything. I played with his toys a little bit, but then I just went back to bed. I was awake when my mom started screaming from the nursery."

She shook her head. "What do you mean? Yes, that's what really happened. What are you trying to say?" The flames became bleary as tears filled her eyes. "Do you think it was my fault?"

Miranda dug her fists into her eyes, wiping away tears as a wave of sobs overtook her. She allowed herself to cry for a moment, then collected herself suddenly with a deep breath.

"You want to know the truth? The truth is that it might be. I don't know." She leaned forward, covering her face with her hands. "I remember standing by his bed, and I knew he was dead. I looked at my hands like I expected to see blood on them. Why would I do that? Think that?"

Her hands slid up her face, pushing her hair back on her head and holding it. "My hands were clean, but…." she trailed off, remembering the day.

"Maybe if I'd done something, gone to get mother. Anything. Maybe they could have done that breathing thing. CPR. But I didn't tell anybody."

Miranda's chin fell to her chest. She stared at the flames dancing before her for a moment, then closed her eyes. "I was never allowed to play with his things, so that's what I did. I played with his toys while he lay dead in the same room. What kind of monster does that? I should have protected him. He was just a helpless baby."

Her head jerked up as a high-pitched buzz came from the darkness. Tilting her head, she strained to listen, shushing Andy when he tried to talk. "Do you hear that?" she asked. She cleaned her face quickly and looked toward her neighborhood. A tiny flash of red light came to her through the trees. It was far away, but there was definitely something there. She looked up, but the canopy and the darkened sky had become one, making it impossible to see. There were no stars out tonight. There was no moon.

Her mind tried to reason that it was only the light from a distant cell phone tower, just now visible because of the falling leaves, but then she saw it again. This time it was in a different place. Her eyes flew wide, and she gasped as a realization came to her suddenly.

She leaned forward and blew out the candles, splattering the rock with melted wax. "It's a drone. Probably the police. I bet they got heat-seeking radar or whatever it's called." She raked leaves over the candles and scurried over the mound, being careful not to squash Andy. Wedging herself into the back of the lean-to, she pulled the jacket over her head.

She lay still in the darkness, listening for the sound of the drone. When it finally drew close, she held her breath. It made a couple of sweeps above the clearing but then moved on. She waited another half hour before climbing from beneath the shelter.

Her eyes searched the black sky, finding no sign of the drone. She drew in a deep breath and released it slowly. How could she have been so stupid not to consider that someone would use a drone to search the woods? People loved those things.

They'd find her eventually, but she wasn't going to let them take Andy. She'd promised to

keep him safe.
> *He's a dandy.*

Chapter Nine

The park around the corner from his house was a bevy of activity, but Jason Ploughman ignored it. He drove straight to the mobile command center with Fairview Police printed on the side on big blue lettering.

"Anything?" he asked.

The sergeant was close to his own age but thinner, with neatly styled blond hair and wire-rimmed glasses. He looked up from the map on the table in front of him.

"Maybe." He motioned Jason over. "Some kid had his drone up last night and swears he saw a light in this area." He pointed to a small red X drawn on the map. "I saw the footage. It's not high resolution, but there was a light. It was distant, through the trees, and it might have been anything."

"It's something."

The sergeant nodded. "It's something, but we don't know what. It could be anything or nothing. It could have been a glitch. It was a commercially available drone and not an expensive one at that."

"It's more than we have now." Jason perused the map. The park ended at the edge of a large tract of woods. Around the corner, five blocks away, his house backed up to the same woods. If Miranda were in the woods, she'd be in this corner. "It makes sense if you think about it. Our house is here," he pointed to the map. "The sighting was here," he pointed to the X. "Miranda has never been what you'd necessarily call an 'outdoorsy' kid. That's not very deep in the woods."

"It's a mile and a half as the crow flies. If

you're walking the hills and valleys, it's going to feel twice as far."

"So what are we going to do?" Jason asked with a tired sigh. He'd barely slept, and the coffee he'd been drinking since dawn was making him feel jittery.

The sergeant nodded to the window above the table. Jason followed his gaze and found three men preparing to launch the biggest drone he'd ever seen.

"This is on loan to us from Providence P.D. It can search this whole scope of woods in just a couple of hours. If she's in there, it'll find her." He sipped his coffee and wiped his lips with the back of his hand. "Unless she's well hidden."

Jason's eyes narrowed. "Why do you think she'd be hiding?"

"Mister Ploughman, we just have to cover all the bases."

"Bases? What bases?"

"In cases like this, there are always surprises. To be perfectly honest, we don't know if Miranda has run away or if she's simply lost. Abduction seems unlikely, but it's not off the board completely."

Jason waved a hand at the map. "It's obvious that she wandered off and got lost. She probably got turned around and walked the wrong way. Doesn't stuff like that happen all the time?"

The sergeant nodded. "It does. Yes. But so do other things."

"I don't like the tone in your voice. My little girl is missing, and it sounds like you're accusing us of something."

"Mister Ploughman, my only job right now is to recover your daughter. We're covering every avenue to help us do that. I know it's offensive for decent people to hear, but things do happen. Terrible things. We have to be prepared for anything and everything. That's our job."

Jason shook his head. He opened his mouth to speak but closed it. He didn't blame the police. The sergeant was right. Sometimes parents did hurt their kids. They didn't know him. "I'm sorry," he mumbled, sinking into a chair.

"Look, go home. Get some rest. We've got this covered."

Jason stood. "No. I can't not do something. I want to be on another search party. Are you sending any out?"

The sergeant nodded over his shoulder. "One's leaving in half an hour from the northern corner of the park, another from the southern corner near your street. You could probably still catch them if you hurry."

"Good. Thanks." Jason turned and hurried out the door.

The sergeant looked at the small red X on his map and sighed. He knew from experience that today was the day. If they didn't find the girl today, the chances of finding her alive would drop drastically. Outside of an incredible stroke of luck, this was their best shot at finding the girl. He picked up a sheet of paper with a set of coordinates on it and went to meet the drone team.

Virginia sat across the table from her daughter, clutching a cup of coffee with both hands. She'd dogged Susan until she'd eaten a piece of toast and had some coffee. The nourishment brought a little color back to her face, but her eyes were still red and swollen.

"Do you remember much after…it happened?"

"Mom, don't. I don't have the strength for that right now."

"I know, but I've been holding some things in my heart, and I think you need to know them."

"Now?"

Virginia nodded.

"Fine then. To answer your question, no. I don't remember much right after Justin died. It was chaos. Everything was a blur for weeks. Months, really."

"I know. That's why I came. The day it

happened, I came right up. It took a little while, and your friend was here with Miranda."

"Cherlyn," Susan said, naming her friend.

Virginia shrugged. It wasn't important. "Anyway, she was as bad as you were. Y'all were at the hospital or wherever, and she was crying. I told her she could go, and she ran out of here like a scalded dog."

"Does this story have a point, Mom?"

"Anyway, I spent a lot of time with Miranda those first few weeks after it happened. Most of the time, she acted perfectly normal, like nothing had happened. It was kinda nice to forget for a few minutes, you know." Virginia looked down at her coffee and sighed. "But sometimes she'd ask where he was. She tried to say, 'he's a dandy' like I did, but it came out as 'he-a Andy'." Virginia blotted her eyes with a tissue. "Such a precious child."

Susan smiled. "She was a late talker. Caught up quick, though." A dry laugh escaped her.

"This one time, we were coloring, and she

drew a picture of Justin in his crib. His fingernails were painted. I asked her about it, and she said she'd seen his funny fingernails. Susan, she'd colored them blue."

"Blue? Why...." Susan's eyes flew wide, and her mouth dropped open. "You don't think...."

"I never knew what to think. I hid the picture. She never brought it up again, and neither did I."

"There's no way she would have hurt him. She loved playing with him, holding him. I mean, she always wanted to change his clothes, like he was one of her dolls."

"I don't know what happened. Maybe she just found him."

"Maybe? What are you getting at, Mom? They did an autopsy. Nothing was wrong with him."

"I know. That's why I never said anything about it. But...."

"But what?"

"I don't know." Virginia clasped her hands

before her. "When I first got here the day it happened, Miranda was really upset. Sometimes she'd be normal, just playing, then she'd start to cry like the devil and say she was sorry."

"Sorry for what?" Susan asked. She pushed a hand through her tangled hair with a groan.

"In my heart, I always thought that maybe she just found him that morning and didn't know to tell anybody."

Pushing her coffee away, Susan crossed her arms on the table and laid her head on them. "I can't, Mom. I can't even think right now. They said it was SIDS."

Virginia reached across the table and stroked her daughter's hair. "I know what they said, but…."

Susan looked up. "But what?"

"I don't know. Do you think she might have done something…I don't know? Maybe by accident?"

"No." Susan laid her hand back down. "Don't. I can't even think about something like that."

"I looked it up. In cases like this, they want to avoid an in depth autopsy so they can have an open service, you know. Being a baby and all."

"Mom, stop. Okay?" Susan dropped her head to the table again with a long groan.

"Look, say she didn't do anything, even accidentally. There's still a very real possibility that she saw him." Virginia shook as a shudder ran through her. "That picture."

Susan shrugged. "I don't know, mom. I mean, I remember her coming into the room. Things were crazy. We were crazy." Susan shook her head, lost in an unpleasant memory. "We were running around, then the paramedics got here. People were everywhere."

"I know they were, baby. It's just a terrible situation all the way around. For everybody."

Susan pushed her hair back and rested her forehead in the palm of her hand. She stared down at the coffee in her cup, wondering just what Miranda had experienced that morning and how it affected her. Her own memory was made up of bits and pieces, seconds-long snapshots of pain and horror that she wouldn't wish on anyone.

Closing her eyes, she pushed forth tears as a memory swam forward. Days after the funeral, she found Justin's bedroom door open. Miranda was inside, holding one of Justin's baby toys. A stuffed lion with a puffy orange mane that rattled when you shook it.

"No, sweetie," she'd said as she took the toy from Miranda and put it back in the crib. "Don't mess with your brother's things."

"Sarge."

The sergeant went to the small tent draped in a blackout cloth on the top and three sides. Beneath it, the operator sat at the controls, watching a monitor on the table in front of him.

"Might have something here, boss."

The sergeant pushed into the tent behind the

operator, his eyes locked on the screen. The aerial view showed an opening in the forest, revealing a small clearing. Near the edge, a collection of poles jutted from the ground at an angle. "What's that?" he asked.

The operator rotated the camera, focusing on the image. "Looks like deadfall. Could be a crude shelter of some kind. Looks like it's been there a while, though." He pointed to the blanket of leaves covering the angled roof. The camera panned around, searching the small clearing from above the treetops. "What the hell is that?"

The sergeant leaned in, squinting at the small black blob at the other end of the clearing. "Can you zoom in?" The operator nodded, adjusting the camera. Both men leaned in. "What is it? Is it a bear?"

The operator shook his head. "I've never seen a bear around here. Kinda looks like a blanket or something, maybe. Could be a dead turkey or something."

"That doesn't look like a turkey to me."

"Seeing things from this angle can fool you sometimes. It takes some getting used to. Odd shadows."

"Maybe so, but if that's a turkey, it's a damned world record bird. It's way too big." The sergeant squinted. "Can you zoom in more?"

"That's it."

"Can you go lower?"

"It's dangerous. If I hit a limb or something, it could cause a crash. My boss will have my ass in a sling."

"I'll take the blame. I want to know what that is. Go lower." When the operator hesitated, he added, "This might be our only hope of finding that girl. There are no more leads."

The operator sighed, putting the drone into a slow descent. It stopped forty feet off the ground and hovered.

"What the hell is it?" the sergeant asked, squinting to see the black shape. "It's definitely a mass of feathers. Look at that."

"Hey, check this out." The camera panned

up from the black mass on the ground to the tree trunks, stopping on one of the ravens Miranda had hung on the trees. "If they are feathers, I know where they came from."

"Is that a crow?"

"Looks like, or what's left of one." The drone moved closer and hovered. The battered raven hung limply from the tree. One wing was gone completely, the other had been stripped. Bones pressed against the dry hide, now pocked with hundreds of tiny craters where feathers had been.

"Who would do something like that?" the sergeant asked, staring at the bird in shocked horror. With the exception of the head, all the feathers had been plucked from its body. On the breast, the ragged ends of pale bones stuck out from the pallid skin.

"There are some sick people in this world." The camera panned slowly to the left, stopping on another tree and another bird. "Damn. There's more than one of them." He panned the entire clearing, counting the birds as he went. When he got back to where he'd started, he'd counted twenty-seven dead ravens.

"Somebody's been at this a while," the sergeant said with a grimace.

"I just hope they're not the ones who has the little girl."

"Go back to the pile of feathers." The sergeant watched the camera pan back to the black mound. "Move in closer."

"We're in dangerous territory here, sarge. The lower we go, the more likely we're going to hit something."

"Just a little lower." The drone descended another ten feet. "How come they didn't blow away?" he asked. "If someone just stripped the birds and piled them up, they should be scattered all over God's creation by the wind."

"You'd think so." The drone descended ten more feet. "It looks like they're stuck to something."

The sergeant leaned in for a closer look.

"Is it a blanket? What is that?" His eyes narrowed. "We're going to have to get closer."

Miranda made herself wait. She sat in the pile of leaves, tucked in a tight ball beneath the coat of feathers she'd made. The buzz of the drone assaulted her ears, making it hard to think. It was close, but she couldn't tell how close. The drone of the propellers came from everywhere at once. She was going to have to take her chances. If she let it get away, they'd know exactly where she was.

Her fingers tightened around the stick between her feet. It was a nice, sturdy one, long and straight. If the drone were close enough, it would do the job.

She exhaled, emptying her lungs, then took in a deep breath. The smell of her own body was strong, mingling with the scent of the feathers. She'd been waiting a long time, but it was almost over.

She counted to three, then sprang into action. Throwing the coat off as she stood, she turned and leapt into the air, finding the drone behind her. It was well within reach. She grunted through clenched teeth as she swung the stick. The drone tilted to one side and started to rise, trying to evade her, but it was too late. The last foot of the hickory stick struck one of the guides that protected the four propellers. It shattered, and the blade stopped. The drone shot to the left and struck a pine sapling. Needles clogged the propeller, forcing it to stop. It wobbled in the air for another second, then crashed to the ground.

Miranda rushed to it, bringing the stick down hard across the x-shaped body. The sound of plastic breaking filled the air, then the remaining blades stopped turning.

Panting, she watched as a series of clicks came from the drone. When one of the propellers started turning again, she brought the stick down hard across it. There was a high-pitched whirring sound, then the woods were silent again. It was dead.

"What the hell was that?" the sergeant asked, drawing back from the screen, now drenched in static as the feed from the drone failed. "Do you still have the footage?"

"I have what was recorded before the strike."

"Play it back. Now."

The operator made several keystrokes, and the scene changed on the monitor. The drone was hovering above the mass of feathers. "When the guy makes his move, slow it down."

The operator did as he was told, watching the footage with the sergeant. The mass of feathers exploded toward the camera, and a stick suddenly appeared. The drone lurched to one side, changing the view from the attacker to the forest floor. The camera jerked violently, spinning in a half circle. The angle changed again, showing one of the dead birds, then it was gone. The camera swept to the left and hit something, shaking the image. A flash of static swallowed the screen, then the view was back. The view on the screen spun, then tilted as the drone fell.

An image flashed on the screen for an instant, then was gone. "Stop," the sergeant instructed, pointing at the screen. "Back it up. Go frame by frame."

The operator complied. Clicking the keyboard to manually advance the scenes one by one. He saw the bird again, then the forest floor, then the trunk of a pine tree, the forest floor, then the attacker. He stopped on the image.

The sergeant leaned in again, studying the image. The face before his was contorted by rage, scarcely resembling the girl they were looking for. Her eyes were squinted, and her lips pulled back from her teeth in an angry scowl. Black hair hung in tangled ropes about her dirty face.

"I don't think it's a guy, sarge."

He pulled a photo from his breast pocket and looked at it. Shaking his head, he looked at the screen. It was the same person, but not at the same time. He looked between the screen and the picture in his hand, wondering how someone could go from being one to the other without it being noticed. The distance between the two images felt like a thousand miles.

"Sarge, if you don't mind, I need to make a call and report this."

The sergeant nodded. "Yeah. Get me those coordinates. I think we've found our missing girl."

The operator stretched to look at the picture in the sergeant's hand. He shook his head, grimacing. "Damn. It doesn't look much like the same girl."

The sergeant sighed, thumbing the photograph. "I think the little girl in this picture has been missing for a long time."

Chapter Ten

Miranda heard the tell-tale signs of their advance. A twig snapping. The crunch of a leaf. An occasional quiet grunt. They weren't the loud, plodding volunteers. They were moving through the woods with a rehearsed precision, surrounding the tiny clearing.

She shook her head, crying as she kneeled next to Andy's grave. "They might not find you. I'll come back to see you. I promise. I don't know when, but I will." She squeezed her eyes shut. "No. They won't let me stay. They're going to take me away. I'll never see you again."

He's a dandy.

Miranda shook her head as sobs wracked her body. "He's not a dandy. He's Andy. Andy. Andy!" she cried, doubling over until her head rested on the grave.

They were close now, but she didn't care. She was going to spend every last second with Andy that she could. Soon he'd be gone forever, and she'd never see him again.

"Miranda." Susan's voice was little more than a hoarse whisper as she spoke her daughter's name. She took a step toward her child, but the sergeant grabbed one arm, and Jason took hold of the other. They'd seen the footage. The police said that she was dangerous and unstable. But all Susan saw was her little girl, and she was crying.

"I'm so sorry, Mama." Miranda sat up, turning her face to the sky. Tears flowed down her cheeks. "I just wanted to play, but he wouldn't wake up. I thought I'd get in trouble. I was so scared." She wrapped her arms around herself and began rocking. "You were so sad, Mama. I'm sorry. I didn't know what to do."

Susan tore from the men and rushed down the incline, skidding to a stop beside her daughter. Miranda looked up at her mother, and her sobs erupted again. "I'm sorry, mommy. I didn't mean to. I didn't."

Susan sank to her knees, gathering Miranda in her arms. "It's okay, baby. It's okay. Mama's here." She held Miranda to her as her own tears began to flow. "It's okay, baby. It's okay."

Jason tore his eyes from his wife and daughter. His eyes went to the crude shelter in front of them. A stuffed animal was nestled in the mound of dried leaves. Its orange mane stood out like a beacon in the sea of brown. His exhausted mind groped for recognition. It might have been one of Justin's. There was a complete set. A lion, a zebra. Maybe a giraffe?

Shaking his head, he pulled his eyes from his family and surveyed the clearing. He recoiled when he saw the first bird, now little more than a loose collection of bones and leathered skin.

His face contorted in anguish as his mind tried to make sense of what he saw. Had Miranda done this? How much had she suffered through in silence?

She'd made a home where she could escape the reality that haunted her or to let it loose. His heart sank as his eyes looked from bird to bird. A hand went to his mouth as his eyes fell on the only bird still intact.

It hung on a tree close to Miranda, wings outstretched. Twine had been wound around its beak, holding its mouth closed tightly. This one would tell no tales.

"What's up with the crows?" the sergeant asked quietly.

Jason shook his head, still touring the

macabre display. His eyes landed on a slingshot hanging on a branch, and his mind retrieved a memory. It played out like a flash in his mind. It was the day he'd taught Miranda how to shoot a slingshot. She'd taken right to it, hitting the empty cans within minutes of starting.

He sighed and looked back at his wife and daughter. It was the one memory he could recall of him and Miranda spending time together. He admitted to himself that the loss of his son had affected him more than he thought. The years since were a blur. He'd formed habits to protect himself, work, golf, and fishing. But all he managed to do was abandon his daughter to fend for herself.

Turning back to the emotional outpouring between his wife and daughter, he thumbed a tear from his own cheek. "They're not crows," he finally said. "They're ravens."

"What's the difference?"

"A flock of crows is called 'a murder.' A flock of ravens is called 'an unkindness.' There's about as much difference as there can be." He staggered down the incline and kneeled next to his family, wrapping his arms around them both.

Low, gray clouds hung over the cemetery, encouraging a biting wind that greeted Miranda as she made her way between the tombstones. The cold bit at her bare fingers clutching the bundle of artificial sunflowers.

Her eyes swept over the faded bouquets and aged stones as she navigated the cemetery. Her heart pounded nervously against her chest. She hadn't been able to visit Andy in months, but it wasn't her fault.

The time since they'd found her in the woods was a blur of meetings. There were meetings with police, lawyers, doctors, counselors, and psychologists. Everyone wanted to talk about Andy. She thought it ironic that if the same people had been half as concerned about him before, she might have never met him.

Miranda made her way to a small, leafless tree and a thin smile came to her lips. Gray rectangles of brown sod lay atop the fresh dirt like a patchwork quilt. That was good. He would always be safe now.

The toes of Miranda's sneakers stopped just short of the grave. Her eyes swept up to the stone bearing a name and the dates that spanned his short life. He'd died two months and two weeks short of his tenth birthday. She sighed. It wasn't much time to enjoy life, but some had gotten much less.

Kneeling on the cold ground, she placed the flowers in the small vase attached to the base of his stone. The bright yellow flowers shone like the sun against the white granite. "Hello, Andy. I brought you some flowers." The wind gusted, sweeping a tear across her cheek. "I picked them out myself. I hope you like them."

Another gust of wind brought the faint squawk of a bird. She looked up, finding a dark bird sitting high in a naked tree at the far edge of the cemetery. As she watched, the bird took flight, heading away from them. Miranda drew in a deep breath and watched until the overcast sky swallowed it.

Her eyes dropped to the stone. Most of what had happened had been kept from the news. She'd been credited with finding the body, and the lawyers said that her statement would go a long way to making sure the parents would pay for what they'd done. But none of that mattered to her. Nobody understood why she'd done what she did. That didn't matter, either. She knew, and Andy knew. She'd taken care of him when he needed it most. Nothing else mattered.

Her eyes traced the name carved into the stone. It said his name was Marshall McClain, but that didn't fit him. He'd always be Andy to her. A tear escaped her as she stood. She let it roll down her cheek as she stared at the grave.

"Everything's going to be okay. You're safe now, Andy." Miranda wiped tears from her cheek. "Good-" her words caught in her throat. A hand went to her mouth as she struggled to regain her composure. Finally, she closed her eyes, pushing more tears down her cheeks. "I've got to go now." Her lips quivered as she looked down at the bright flowers.

Miranda tore herself from the grave and turned to leave but stopped suddenly. She wiped a tear from her cheek and turned back. "Goodbye, Andy. Thanks for being my friend."

John Ryland lives and writes in Northport, Alabama with his wife and two sons. His previous works include the novels *Souls Harbor* and *Shatter*, the collection of short stories entitled *Southern Gothic*, and a poetry chapbook, *The Stranger, Poems from the chair*. You can find his other works in publications such *as Bewildering Stories, The Eldritch Journal, The Writer's Magazine, Otherwise Engaged, The Birmingham Arts Journal, Subterranean Blue*, and others, as well as the online journal *The Chamber Magazine*. His novel *The Man with No Eyes* was released in March 2022.

When not writing or attending various sporting events for his sons, he enjoys gardening, people watching, and wondering what makes people do the things they do.

Made in the USA
Columbia, SC
01 August 2023